A Different Life Lived

Rebecca Gertner

www.ADifferentLifeLived.com

The Strength To Stand Series
www.TheStrengthToStand.com

Creative Team Publishing
San Diego

Disclaimer:

The story and all characters depicted in this book are fiction. All facts depicted in the book are a creation of fiction or taken from public record and national headlines. Any resemblance to any known or real person, fact, circumstance, event, or situation is purely coincidental.

Resources:

- Study Questions can be found on page 297. The Study Questions were created to facilitate those who wish to use this book for group discussion or self-reflection.
- Information concerning Human Trafficking and Sex Trafficking can be found on page 299. If you are a victim of trafficking or become aware of someone who is, please contact your local police authority. Do not attempt a victim rescue on your own.
- Products and Services can be found on page 303.

ISBN: 978-0-9903398-1-6
PUBLISHED BY CREATIVE TEAM PUBLISHING
www.CreativeTeamPublishing.com
San Diego
Printed in the United States of America

Dedication

For my children — Karsten, Faith, and Grace —
who continually remind me
that sometimes the greatest work
we can do for God
is found right in our very own homes.

May my life and heart reflect the love and dedication
I have for each of you!

December 1992

Violet's pulse pounded in her veins, and her feet were pounding on the ground. With all the events of the last few weeks swirling in her head, Violet tried to focus on the two main things—the fact that she was alive and free, and the fact that she needed to keep running to insure she would remain alive and free.

The reality that she had been kidnapped was something she couldn't process right now. It didn't seem possible that she would have gotten caught up in something so dangerous. Yet, if she looked past the surface, Violet knew she would see all the warning signs her heart hadn't wanted to acknowledge about her exciting life in Mexico. *How could I have been so stupid?*

With each panicked step, Violet had to force herself not to look back. Was she being followed? What if she were caught? The exertion of running had exhausted her and she knew her chances of fighting off another attack were pitiful. It had been hard enough to free herself from his strong arms the first time, even with the fresh burst of adrenaline. Now, however, her adrenaline was wearing off, and shock was setting in. Her teeth were chattering and she was freezing cold, even as she felt the sweat beading up on her forehead.

I just have to get to The Mission... just a little farther... The Mission... then I'll be ok.

Suddenly, Violet was aware of a ticking sound. Fear raced down the back of her neck as she imagined all sorts of different things that could be making the sound. Keys jangling in her captor's pocket as he ran after her? Or was it bullets in his pocket? Was she going to be shot?

When Violet found herself sprawling toward the ground, she tried to make the impact of the street be on her hands instead of her head. But the action was too late, and with a muffled cry, she landed flat on her face. Stunned, she lay there for a second trying to breathe, mentally taking inventory to see what was hurt. *Am I shot? Is that what happened?*

Thankfully, the only searing pain she felt was in her already damaged arm. With a sigh of relief, she realized she hadn't heard the bang of a gunshot, either. Rolling to her side, Violet tried to push herself up with her good arm. Gasping in agony, she quickly realized that even though her face had taken the brunt of the impact, she had hurt her wrist as she tried to break her fall—now both of her arms suffered injury.

Her second try was successful and as Violet sat up, she saw that she was missing a shoe. Gingerly touching her already swelling eye, she saw the bright green shoe a few feet away from her. In her panic to get away, she had forgotten that her shoes were untied. And apparently, the untied laces had been lashing against the street, making the sound she had heard — until she had tripped herself on them. The fact that she would do something as impractical as running with untied shoes bothered her. *Just one more thing to prove my stupidity.*

Fearing the fall had cost her precious time, Violet jumped to her feet and started running. She didn't stop to retrieve the shoe that had come off. She was too scared and too dazed from the blow to her head to care. All she could think about was getting away from it all.

No one could ever know what had happened. If anyone ever found out, the ramifications would be too great.

I have to get home... no one can know what I did to deserve this.

Chapter 1

April 1994

"You're doing what?" Shawn asked, as he took a step closer to Violet.

Violet Thompson stood with her shoulders squared and her chin held at a stubborn angle. She realized the conversation wasn't going to go as well as she had hoped, but it was important. She also knew that no matter what Shawn said, she was not going to change her mind.

"I'm going back to Mexico. I really... " Violet was ready to defend her choice, but Shawn cut her off mid-sentence.

"No! It's out of the question." Shawn Sinclair's years in the police force had resulted in a tough exterior. Those years had also given him a tendency to speak with authority, even when he didn't have that right. "The last time you went to that Mission you were kidnapped. You're not going back." When Violet started to interrupt, Shawn put his hand up to silence her. "I won't allow it. It's my job as your fiancé to keep you safe and so I'm telling you no."

"Shawn, please, you don't understand. I won't be in any danger... " Violet sighed and closed her large brown eyes, trying to keep her tears from falling. "You have to trust me; I know what I am doing. I wouldn't go back if I thought it was dangerous."

"You're right! I don't understand! But how can I if you never give me the chance?" Shawn was pacing now. He walked back and forth between his desk and the door to his office. His frustration was obvious when he slammed the door shut, lending their argument more privacy. "You ask me to trust you, but you don't trust me! If you did, you would tell me what happened when you were kidnapped."

"How many times do we have to go over this?" Violet was shouting now. From the day they had started dating Shawn had been trying to get her to tell him the details of that fateful trip to Mexico. The strain of keeping such a secret from the man she loved was weighing on her, but she couldn't tell. No one would ever look at her the same, not to mention the danger that exposing such a secret would unleash. "I simply cannot tell you. I'm sorry. I do trust you; I'm going to marry you, aren't I?"

"Maybe you're not. What happens if you go there and get yourself kidnapped again? Shoot, you could get raped and murdered for all I know! From all the evidence we have, it appears as if Frank escaped the police and has disappeared across the border."

Violet wanted to stomp her feet and scream. Was that all Shawn thought about? "I can't do this. I am not having another conversation about Frank Smith!"

Ever since Violet's best friend, Rachel Riley, had been stalked by Frank, Shawn had become obsessed with bringing Frank to justice. "Look, I know you were angry when Frank was found not guilty at the trial. And I know you were even angrier when he beat up Rachel's boyfriend. I was, too! How can a person not get angry over such needless violence? I sobbed over the damage Frank had caused. And when he disappeared, I also got angry, so angry that I kicked the chair and broke my toe!" Violet walked over and placed her hand on Shawn's arm. It was a gesture of peace in a volatile moment, a gesture that showed Violet was trying to calm them both down. "But honey, you have to think about something else. I can't live like this. Everything you do, everything I do," Violet swept her arm, gesturing at the whole room, "everything that happens... makes you think about Frank in some way. You live as if the only thing that matters is to find him."

As the words came out of Violet's mouth, she could see the tension building within Shawn. With an angry motion, he pulled away from her touch. "You have no idea! You say I don't understand about you wanting to go to Mexico! Well, you don't understand me! I'm not stupid, Violet." Shawn's eyes were flashing, his stocky body tense as if he were ready to fight off an attacker. "People like him don't deserve to go free! And people like Rachel don't deserve to be treated the way he treated her! If only the stupid jury wouldn't have believed those lies and struck my witness from the record! I was the only ally Rachel had in the police force and I was rendered helpless. Rachel needed me and I failed her. But I'm working my hardest to make sure that doesn't happen again."

Sadness filled Violet's eyes. "But what about me? What about my dreams? Must they die because of the stupidity of one perverted man?"

"What about you?" Shawn's disbelief was apparent in his reaction, showing Violet that he was shocked by her question. "That's what I'm trying to tell you! I'm protecting you! How can you ask me that question? I'm putting you and your safety first."

"No Shawn, you're putting your vendetta first."

"What a messed up way to see things! I love you more than I can say, Violet, I really do. But right now, I'm just not seeing how this is going to work." Shawn's whole body seemed to droop in defeat.

Feeling relieved that maybe Shawn was seeing how useless his argument was, Violet looked up at him and dared to smile the faintest of smiles. "You're right, arguing won't work. I'm going back to Mexico."

"No. That's not what I meant," he whispered. "Us… me and you. I just can't see this working."

"You don't mean that! Tell me you're just angry and frustrated." Tears blurred Violet's vision. "Tell me you didn't mean it!"

Shawn had begun to walk away from Violet, and she wondered what she was supposed to do. They had fought before, but they had never talked about splitting up. With searing pain squeezing her heart, Violet couldn't let him go. She loved him, she needed him. "Shawn, stop. Please." She cried as she followed him.

Shawn stopped walking and stood with his back toward her. When she reached out to touch his shoulder, he turned suddenly and wrapped her in his arms and kissed her golden blonde head. "Oh, Vi, I love you so much. Please don't do this to me. How could a marriage between us ever work if the very foundation is built on lies?"

Violet pulled back from his embrace just enough to look into his eyes. "Lies? I'm confused. When have I lied to you?"

"You refuse to talk to me about your past. What am I supposed to do with that? You say you were kidnapped, but you also insist that returning to the place it happened poses no danger to you. It's too simple an explanation. There's more to the story and since you keep the truth hidden away, I'm left to fight with my imagination about what might have taken place. You could have chosen to run off with some creep and then changed your mind for all I know!"

Wrestling out of Shawn's arms, Violet pushed him away in a display of anger. The imaginations he had mentioned came too close to reality. She couldn't stay near him and deny the shred of truth in what he suggested, she would lose her resolve. She had to get away before she opened up Pandora's Box by telling Shawn the details of that terrible day. *When did life get so complicated?*

"You're right." She said as she turned to leave. "This isn't going to work. I'm not lying to you, but you think I am. All I am doing is trying to move on and not live in the past. You, however, don't want to move on. You want to bring my kidnapping and Frank Smith into a marriage that hasn't even started yet." Violet stopped mid-step and turned back to Shawn. With a single tear rolling down her cheek, she pulled the beautiful engagement ring off her finger. Her hands trembled as she placed it in Shawn's large, calloused hand.

Shawn grabbed hold of her fingers, refusing to let her go. "Wait, I didn't mean it. Please, don't take the ring off. We can work this out." His voice broke on the last word and whatever else he was going to say was left to her speculation as he pushed his lips into a tight, thin line. His effort not to cry wasn't successful and large tears traced a trail down his freckled cheeks and dripped off his chin. His face, flushed with emotion, matched his red hair.

"I love you." She choked out the words. "But I have to go."

Violet ran; she ran as fast as she could. She didn't trust herself to simply walk. Her broken heart would drive her back to him. As she left the police station, she marveled at how quickly life can change. When she had walked through the door just an hour earlier, she was filled with excitement. They were supposed to have gone out for dinner, but instead they ended up breaking each other's hearts.

Chapter 2

The air was too stuffy, the seat too small, and the person next to her was too big. Normally, Violet loved to fly, but not today because nothing felt normal to her—for the simple reason that nothing was normal. Somehow, over the course of the past few days, she had alienated herself from every important person in her life. First, she had called off her engagement to Shawn. Then, in a fit of anger, she had ruined her friendship with Rachel. When she had called Rachel after her fight with Shawn, Violet had wanted a sympathetic ear. But what she had got was a lecture about needing to tell people what had happened in Mexico. Violet still could not understand why everyone insisted on making such a big deal about it. Sure, they all cared about her and her safety. But why couldn't they just trust her? She was making the right choice by going back to The Mission. She was certain of it.

There were some things, however, that made her question her choice to escape the drama at home by leaving today. After having an argument with not only Rachel and Shawn, but her parents as well, Violet decided to leave for Mexico early.   What difference would one month make anyway?   It wasn't like she was going to decide to tell Shawn all the stupid little details of her kidnapping, and Shawn wasn't going to give up on his obsessive search for Frank. There was no fixing the mess they had made in their relationship. *If only Shawn wasn't so stubborn!*

The discomfort of her flight caused her anger to rise. She didn't want to admit the reason she found herself on such a cramped plane was due to her rash decision to leave early. It wasn't easy to get a flight the same day you wanted to leave, and so, it was a tiny plane filled with loud, annoying people that carried her away from her problems.

Since the man next to her was insisting on making small talk, Violet pulled her Bible out of her carry-on luggage. Opening it to 1 Corinthians, she turned in her chair as much as possible to silently tell the man next to her that she wasn't interested in chatting. Even though she wasn't really in the mood to read, she began to read anyway. As she started reading the 13th Chapter, she had to laugh at the irony of how her daily study routine had brought her to the most famous passage in the Bible about love. How could she read about love when she was so brokenhearted?   *Are you speaking to me, God?*

With lips that moved ever so slightly, she read;

"Love is patient, love is kind. It does not envy, it does not boast, it is not proud. It does not dishonor others, it is not self-seeking, it is not easily angered, it keeps no record of wrongs. Love does not delight in evil but rejoices with the truth. It always protects, always trusts, always hopes, always perseveres."

Sadness wrapped around her heart. Did she even truly know how to love? She certainly wasn't being kind or patient with Shawn. And maybe his reason for wanting her to stay home really was because he loved her. After all, it said that love always protects. Didn't he tell her he was only trying to protect her?

Frustration boiled up inside her heart and she slammed the Bible shut. If God was trying to speak to her, it was too late. She was already halfway to the San Diego airport by now, and from there, it was a mere hour drive before she would reach her destination. There was no changing her mind; she was supposed to be in Mexico. She had been dreaming of this day her whole life. And now that it was finally here, she wasn't going to let anything ruin the joy of fulfilling her life-long dream. It may have taken her longer than she had thought it would, but 25 was still a young age. And honestly, she hadn't met many full-time missionaries who were fresh out of school anyway.

With no desire at all to read more, and no desire to think about what God might be telling her concerning her broken relationships back home, Violet reclined her seat the luxurious two inches an airline seat goes back and tried to sleep. The man sitting next to her was bumping around, and the little baby across the aisle was screaming, but somehow she managed to doze off.

· ∘ ●◉● ∘ ·

"What do you mean it's lost?" Violet was on the verge of tears.

"I'm sorry ma'am, but we cannot find your luggage." The man in the uniform sounded more bored than sorry.

"How in the world did you lose my luggage when there wasn't even a connecting flight? I got on the plane and it took me here!"

"Maybe it didn't get on the plane in the first place… I don't know."

Violet took a deep breath and reminded herself that she was a Missionary now and Missionaries didn't yell at people. "Can you please find out what happened? I am going to Tijuana and I need my luggage."

With a sigh, and what Violet swore was an eye roll, the attendant promised to check into it if she would take a seat. Without any other choice, Violet found a seat near the front desk where she had gone to ask about her luggage and sat down. People crowded the busy airport and she tried to relax as she watched the crowd. Some of the people ran around as if they were late for their flight, while others seemed to have all the time in the world. *It's odd how we are all here at the same time, but our lives are so varied. I wonder how many of them are happy… do any of them feel as frustrated with life as I do?*

There were old people and young people, families with small children, and business professionals. But what Violet noticed most was how the people traveling alone smiled less than those with a companion. It was an innocent observance, but soon the thought turned malicious as it reminded her of how isolated she was right now.

She was deep in thought when the same unenthusiastic man walked up to her. "Ma'am, I've been making calls, but I still don't know where your luggage is. Did you have your name on it?"

"Yes, I had the luggage tag filled out and attached to the handle."

"Well, then you will just have to wait for it to be sent to your home." The man smiled a relieved smile and turned to leave. Violet wondered if he was smiling because she had the tag on the suitcase or because he was walking away. Customer service was not one of the man's strong points, but he had done his job. And why should she take out her frustration on him when he wasn't the one who forgot to put her suitcase onto the plane?

Taking weary steps, Violet walked out the door and tried to make a plan. "I have no luggage... I didn't have time to contact The Mission, so no one will be here to pick me up... and now I need to send a note to mom and dad so they don't worry when my suitcase arrives back home..." Violet's practical side was kicking in as she muttered the details of her situation.

In a matter of minutes, she had decided to use the modest amount of money she had in her purse to hire a cab to take her shopping and then to the border. Then, she would hire another cab once she was in Mexico to take her to

The Mission. If she was careful, she would have enough money to buy a sufficient wardrobe and still hire the cabs.

When she stepped out of the mall an hour later, she had several shopping bags clutched in her hand. Because her stay at The Mission was going to be indefinite, Violet decided to forgo the purchase of a new suitcase. When the time came for her to return home, she was sure to find something at one of the shops near The Mission. She had originally planned to work there only for half a year, but with the end of her engagement, Violet had decided to be one of the full-time volunteers.

Flagging the taxi that was waiting for her, she mentally readied herself for the emotions the next hour was sure to bring. It may have been over a year since the first time she had made that journey, but the stark contrast between the wealth of the U.S. and the poverty of Tijuana was embedded in her memory forever.

After the U.S. taxi took her to the border, she went through the necessary procedures and then climbed into a Mexican taxi to begin the final stretch of her trip. As they drove, she noticed once again how abrupt a change there was when leaving the States and entering Mexico. Even though the border areas of the U.S. weren't exactly the nicest, they were considerably nicer than the streets just past the border. Graffiti covered every wall of the unkempt buildings. Broken liquor bottles littered the streets and it bothered Violet to see barefooted little children running around. Just the thought of how quickly one of those shards of glass could cut open tiny feet made her stomach turn and she had to look away.

Staring down at her own feet, Violet saw the bright pink tennis shoes she had purchased for this trip. When a strange tingle ran through her stomach, she tried to push down the memory of what had happened to her favorite pair of shoes — the bright green pair she had bought for her first trip to The Mission. After leaving one shoe in the street, she had taken off the other and thrown it in a trash can. Running from her kidnapper with one shoe on and one shoe off was too much trouble and holding the shoe had proven cumbersome. And so, not only had she lost a piece of her innocence that day, she had lost her favorite shoes.

Shaking her head a little, she looked out the window again just in time to see The Mission off in the distance. The familiar sight took her breath away as it filled her mind with memories.

Chapter 3

November 1992

She was still in shock from the images that had just assaulted her eyes. Violet had known the city of Tijuana had slums and areas of poverty, but she had been mentally picturing them like the bad areas of Los Angeles or San Diego. In reality, it didn't really compare, and that knowledge left her with a feeling of discomfort. But the discomfort wasn't because of the city; it was the people, and more specifically, the children. They ran and played, they laughed and smiled. They seemed almost more content than the children in the U.S. *We are a spoiled nation and don't even know it. And if we do know, does it change anything about us? Do we care?*

As the pastor of The Mission pulled his car into the dirt parking lot, he explained to Violet how The Mission had originally started in his home. "My wife and I felt like God was calling us to serve Him in Mexico and so one day I just quit my job in the States and we moved here. That was twenty years ago."

Violet could easily imagine why a person would do such a thing. She had felt the strong pull to serve in Mexico as well. And she was grateful for people like Pastor Paul Larkson and his wife, Anna, who answered the call and paved the way for her to be on the mission field today.

"In those twenty years we have seen so many children come and go through our doors. Anna was never able to have a child of her own, so she was determined to love every child that came our way. At first we were heartbroken because we couldn't take in all the children who needed us. But eventually we were able to purchase the old hospital next door to our house and turn it into the school and boardinghouse you see today." Paul looked at the large building with pride. "Oh, what the Lord can do when His people listen and work together. A very large donation has not only allowed us to purchase the building, it also gave us the funds we needed to do the necessary remodeling and also gave us a reserve of money to spend where needed. We can now buy things like food, clothes, and schooling materials without wondering where the money will come from."

Violet couldn't speak; she was so focused on the sights before her. The Mission was a faded blue three story building. The actual footprint of the old hospital wasn't very large, but since it was three stories, the building was quite impressive. Finally finding her voice she said, "Pastor Paul! This is amazing, so much more than I expected."

"We are blessed indeed. And we are even more blessed to have you here with us for the next few weeks. The world needs more young people like you — individuals who are uncompromising and full of Godly morals and desires. You're one of those rare people who make the world a better place."

"You're too kind," Violet muttered. "I'm just trying my best." Although his words were meant as a compliment, Violet couldn't help but feel reprimanded more than complimented. *What would Pastor Paul think if he knew the truth? I'm not uncompromising, I've simply built walls around myself to keep the temptations out... If he only knew the things I've thought about.*

· · ●●◉●● · ·

"And this is our playground," Anna, Pastor Paul's wife, said as they ended their tour of the campus. Anna had taken Violet to the top floor of The Mission first. It was obvious that some walls had been taken down and the floor plan was changed from the original design. But the result was a wonderful open feel, and Violet instantly felt drawn to the environment that had been created. It was a place where imagination was stimulated by large colorful paintings on the walls. Giant numbers and letters hung from the ceiling, and the children's artwork was on display.

The second story was the dormitory and Violet was surprised to see fifteen very tidy rooms; the cleanliness of those rooms spoke of the structure of The Mission. The rooms had also been larger than Violet had expected; each with a set of bunk beds, a dresser and a small bathroom— thanks to the building having originally been a hospital.

While on the second floor, Anna had shown Violet the living quarters that she and Paul occupied, as well as the student room down the hall that Violet was going to stay in. Although Violet loved children, she breathed a sigh of relief to know she didn't have to share her room. A place to call her own would be nice.

Then, after looking at the kitchen, dining hall, and great room on the ground floor, Anna had taken Violet out to watch the children play on the playground.

Violet watched the antics of the nineteen children, ranging in ages from four to sixteen, and smiled. "They look so happy, Anna!"

Anna smiled. "I would like to think it's because they actually are!"

Hearing the children call to each other in English, Violet said, "I really like how The Mission is bi-lingual. What an advantage you are giving these kids!"

"That was Paul's idea. He's a smart one, he is. He wanted the children to have the freedom to choose their future. Some of them will stay here in Mexico, and that is wonderful. But others... others will want to see what the U.S. has to offer, and so they will be prepared. It's hard going to a country where you don't speak the language."

Violet laughed, "I'm starting to see the truth of that statement already!" Although she knew God was calling her to missions, Violet hadn't known where until recently. And since learning a second language had proved to be harder than she had thought it might be, Violet had procrastinated when it came to learning Spanish. She knew a few words, but not nearly enough to actually communicate. It was just one more reason why she had pursued coming to The Mission: their bi-lingual focus made life much easier for her.

"Anna, why is this orphanage and school simply called The Mission? Why not some other name to give it distinction?"

"I hate the word 'orphanage.' It seems so cold and gives the children a feeling of being unwanted. So I refused to let the people call it that. Paul used to laugh and say I was a woman on a mission to make every child feel loved and wanted. And so, over the course of a year or so, as we would discuss different names, none of them appealed to us. One day, it seemed to dawn on Paul to just call it The Mission. What was the point of naming the place anyway? Everyone in Tijuana knew what we did here, and they all simply called it The Mission. We weren't about to call it The Larkson House or anything like that. The last thing we would want to do is have people think of us when they thought of the work done here. We want God to be seen, His love and care, and all that He has to offer."

"The Mission," Violet said in a whisper. "Simple, yet lovely. What a testimony you and Paul are. I'm sure I will learn a lot about humility and having a servant's heart from the two of you."

Anna reached over and caressed Violet's blonde hair. "Oh child, we always have a lot to learn; even an old woman in her fifties like me!"

Normally the touch of a stranger was uncomfortable for Violet, but there was something different about Anna. Even though they had just met, Violet felt as if she had known her for a long time and the loving caress fed Violet's soul. It was no wonder why the children loved her so and called her "Mamá."

As the two women spent the day getting to know each other, Violet knew she had found a hidden treasure in Tijuana. Anna Larkson was the mentor Violet had been praying for God to send her.

Chapter 4

April 1994

Apprehension made Violet almost ill as she opened the car door and stepped out. Tensions were high when Violet had left The Mission the day of her kidnapping over a year ago. Although Pastor Larkson had extended forgiveness to Violet for her indiscretion, there was a small part of her that wondered what he really thought. When she had contacted him concerning her return, there was obvious hesitation on his part. But at the time, the only thing that mattered to her was that he had agreed to let her come back. Now, however, the idea seemed a little harebrained. As much as she hated to admit it, maybe everyone was right. Maybe she shouldn't be here right now; but not because she was in danger of being kidnapped again. No, she knew that wasn't the issue. What she was in danger of was seeing Anna's disappointment in her; and with the fragile state of her heart, Violet didn't think she could handle that. Since Anna had been running errands that terrible day when Violet had run back to The Mission, Violet had not seen her reaction upon learning about what Violet had gotten involved in. Pastor Larkson had insisted it was vital to her safety, and the safety of the children at The Mission, to get Violet back into the States as soon as possible. It had broken Violet's heart not to be able to say goodbye to her cherished mentor, but she had also felt a measure of relief.

As Violet pulled her shopping bags out of the trunk of the cab, she wished she could be spared the embarrassment she was sure to feel as Anna chided her for being so foolish. She was prepared to promise to be wiser this time and to make them proud, but would it be enough?

After paying the taxi driver, Violet squared her shoulders and walked to the door as if she had all the confidence in the world. *It's a good thing I can fake it. I may be terrified on the inside, but at least no one has to know.*

After knocking on the solid wood door, Violet smiled as she heard the chatter of children grow quiet at the sound. Rapid-fire Spanish was followed by directions in English, resulting in the clunking of children running up the stairs. Violet glanced at her wristwatch and noticed it was a little after noon. The early morning flight had left her feeling as if it were closer to dinner time than lunch. If the staff held the same schedule, lunch was already finished and the children were returning to their studies now. Violet figured it would be a good time of the day for her to show up unannounced and was grateful that at least something had turned out well today.

While Violet stood waiting for someone to answer the door, she nervously clenched her hands. When she heard the sound of crinkling plastic bags, she became aware of the fact that she was holding all her possessions. Feeling awkward, and reminded of the lost luggage and frustrations of the day, Violet set the bags down. At least the hard part of the day was over. Now all she had to do was fall back into the routine here and win over the hearts of the children. Giggling a little, she thought she just might work a little harder to learn Spanish this time.

The door opened with a loud squeak and Violet was stunned to see Anna standing in the doorway. Wearing the same faded apron, Anna looked exactly the same as she had remembered. Seeing Violet standing there apparently was a surprise and Violet watched with sadness as the bright smile on Anna's face was replaced with a frown. But just as quickly as it had disappeared, the smile returned.

"Violet! What a surprise." Anna stepped back and motioned for Violet to enter. "Paul mentioned you were coming back, but he didn't tell me it would be so soon!"

As if wondering what to do, Anna waited for Violet to step fully inside, then in an impulsive act, she wrapped Violet in her arms. "Oh! My dear, sweet child!"

The strain of the day had taken its toll on Violet and without really understanding why, she found herself clinging to Anna as a sob escaped from her lips.

"Oh my, what is this? What are these tears for?" Anna asked as she rubbed Violet's back in a comforting motherly fashion.

"It's been a terrible couple of days. Shawn won't marry me. Rachel hates me. And to top it off, I lost all my belongings when the airline lost my luggage!" Violet knew she was exaggerating, but she didn't have any desire to correct her complaint.

Anna let go of Violet, and looked into her teary eyes. A knowing passed between them. Anna knew there was more to the story than people simply deciding they didn't like her. But true to her character, Anna extended compassion instead of judgment, and that action gave Violet hope that maybe Anna would extend just as much mercy when they talked about the kidnapping. "That sounds terrible indeed! Come inside and I will get you some nice, cold horchata."

Violet did as she was told. Following Anna into the kitchen and then taking a seat at the small table in the corner, Violet was able to stop her tears.

"There you go! With an extra dash of cinnamon on top, just the way you like it."

Violet gratefully took the cloudy white rice drink from Anna's hand and took a sip. "Mmmm, no one makes it as good as you do, Anna. I've missed your cooking."

Anna acknowledged the compliment with a wave of her hand as she took a seat across the table from Violet. "So, are you going to tell me about all your troubles?"

Violet spent the next twenty minutes sharing all the ugly details of her dissolved relationships. She even told Anna about the passage of scripture she had read on the flight.

Once she was finished, she knew what Anna was going to say.

"So why haven't you told them what happened?" were the first words out of Anna's mouth.

If she had felt more lighthearted, Violet would have said the words with her, showing Anna she had expected them. "Ah, I knew you would say that."

For a moment, Violet stared at the speckled pattern the cinnamon had made on the top of her drink. When would she be able to stop answering that question? And when would people just accept that there were things she didn't want, or need, to explain? "Anna, don't you have things in your life that are better if they are not talked about?"

"Of course, I have these wayward thoughts here and there. And I know that in Colossians it says our speech is to always be with grace as though it were seasoned with salt. So there are times that I have to choose to stuff down some of the gossip and self-righteous opinions that want to pass through my lips. Those things are better left unsaid, that's for sure."

Again, Anna was showing Violet just how much she could learn from this gentle woman. Letting out a sigh, Violet said, "You make me feel so bad sometimes! Gossip and those things are just some of the many things about me that I feel are better not talked about. I'm not talking about those, though. I'm asking you why it's so darn important for people to know what happened here."

"Why not tell them? You weren't very specific when you told Paul what happened. He said you basically just told him that you had gone into the part of town he had told you to stay away from. He said you admitted how wrong that was, but other than that you refused to talk to him about it. Why?" Anna leaned over the table as if pleading with Violet to open up and speak freely.

"It's the difference between life and death." Violet forced the words out. Never before had she shared how important her silence was. "How can I talk about what happened if the result could lead to something terrible?"

Anna's eyes grew huge. "But why are you here then? How could you come back if you were in danger?"

"I'm not. Trust me, I'm not." Violet sighed. See what talking got her? It was useless, the more she tried to explain, the more she had to say. She simply could not tell people what had happened, it was too dangerous. "Anna, I love you. I respect you, so much. But can we just not talk about this?"

An awkward silence settled over both women. Like all the other things surrounding her return to The Mission, the conversation had turned out to be less desirable than Violet had hoped. Finally, she broke the silence with a timid question. "So, what should I do first, unpack?"

"No." A stern, male voice from the doorway behind Violet answered the question before Anna had time to respond. "Don't bother unpacking; you're not staying here."

Chapter 5

Pastor Paul Larkson stood in the doorway. His slightly rotund belly caused the buttons on his shirt to gape, and the bald patch on his head was shiny. But in spite of these things, Violet could see why Anna had fallen in love with him. He was a handsome man, even if it was in a geeky sort of way.

"Paul, couldn't you break it to her more gently?" Anna's eyes were pleading for him to be nice.

Paul remained in the doorway and made no move to join the women at the table. "Anna, you know that Violet isn't really needed here, not nearly as much as she's needed at the soup kitchen."

Violet looked from Paul and back to Anna, hoping she would gain some shred of information to give her a clue as to what they were talking about. "Soup kitchen?"

"Yes. Since you were here last, there have been several of the..." Paul cleared his voice as if uncomfortable and uncertain of what to say. "You know, the girls... They've been coming here asking for prayer. But we've also had a lot of homeless coming here, too."

Reaching her hand up to smooth her hair, Violet wondered if her face was as red as it felt. Had she been part of the reason the girls working the streets were coming here? And if so, were there other things that had resulted from her actions the last time she was here?

"Do you know why that might be?"

In response to Pastor Paul's question, Violet shook her head no, but the action made her feel just as guilty as if she had spoken an outright lie. She had her ideas of why, but she wasn't going to say them.

"Anyway," he continued, "we cannot bring them here with the children. It just isn't right. So we decided to start a soup kitchen. When people come here for help, we will tell them to go there, instead. Eventually, the word will get out, but for now, we are focusing on getting organized. We want to provide clothing and toiletries as well as food."

"Wait, you can't be serious!" Violet was beginning to panic. She didn't want to work at a soup kitchen! That was the type of thing she could easily do in the States. She came here to mentor children and help change their lives, not ladle soup. Besides, working with adults felt too risky. What if someone recognized her?

"Why wouldn't he be serious, dear?" Anna asked.

Paul looked as if Violet had lost her mind. "The need is great. Of course I'm serious."

"I understand the need is great. But how can you send me there? I need to stay here and work with the children. I'm familiar with that... and... and..." Violet couldn't seem to get her thoughts to come out in words.

Anna got up from her chair, walked over and placed her hand on Violet's shoulder. The touch was reassuring, yet Violet resented the way it made her feel like a small child who was being unreasonable. "Oh Violet, the first thing you need to know about being a missionary is that we are seldom called to be comfortable. The work the Lord has for us always stretches us, always makes us grow."

Those were things Violet understood. Serving meant getting out of your comfort zone and doing things you never thought you would. She also understood the process of growth that resulted from placing yourself in a hard situation to serve others. But what she didn't understand was how she could possibly accomplish what was being asked of her. If the kidnapping hadn't happened, then maybe she could. "I can't. I just can't do this. Please let me stay here."

"Even if I wanted to let you stay, there's nothing for you to do here, Violet. The current volunteer remains here until next month. There's no room for you here and I, as The Mission Pastor, am not going to send someone else to another ministry location because you decided to come here earlier than discussed. It wouldn't be fair."

Everything came back to her rash decision to leave the U.S. early. "Please let me stay?" she tried again. "Why don't you want me to?"

"I don't understand what happened to you. When you arrived here you were level headed and easy to work with. Then, as the days went on, apparently something changed." Walking away from the doorway, Paul came nearer Violet. He knelt down by her chair and placed his hand on the table. His eyes were level with hers and she felt exposed by the way he looked into them. "I never expected you to defy my authority, but you did. And look at what came of that. You have been forgiven your foolishness, but you cannot come here and demand the right to do as you please. Nor can you expect me to allow you to be a mentor to the children. Until you get your heart straightened out, you cannot be allowed to influence the children."

Shame filled Violet and she closed her eyes, hoping to keep Paul from seeing her vulnerability. "Yes sir."

"You have two choices; you can go help Everest at the soup kitchen or you can go home."

Anna squeezed Violet's shoulder. There was no need for Anna to say anything. Violet knew she would agree with anything her husband said; she wasn't just loyal, she trusted his leadership.

With too many ideas and thoughts swirling in Violet's head, formulating a response was difficult. She had so many questions. Where was the new ministry located? Would it bring her near any dangerous places? What would her job be? But if she didn't go, she would have to go home.

Am I ready to go back and face everyone? Could I get past the embarrassment of admitting I was wrong, that I shouldn't have come here in the first place? With trembling lips, Violet opened her mouth to begin asking her many questions, but the words that came out seemed to be spoken by someone else. "Okay. I'll go."

Chapter 6

Tensions were high as Pastor Paul drove Violet to the soup kitchen. Violet wasn't sure what she was thinking; agreeing to work there opened her up to all sorts of problems.

First, unlike The Mission, Mesa Vecindad, which means "neighborhood table" in English, wasn't bi-lingual. Some of the people seeking help there would probably speak a little English, but most of them wouldn't. Violet felt frustrated and wondered how she was going to connect with people and influence them if she couldn't even speak their language.

But that wasn't the main issue she was having. By working at Mesa Vecindad, she was putting herself in a precarious situation. When Violet had first thought about coming back, she had promised herself that she would just stay away from the area of town where she had gotten into trouble. By staying away from that street and all the temptations it had to offer, she was certain to be okay this time around. But here she was, willingly being taken to a location near those places. She had knowingly agreed to be in contact with people from those areas again! *I'm a fool. I shouldn't be doing this...*

"Everest is one of the nicest men I know," Pastor Paul broke the strained silence. "He's the one who really got the soup kitchen to be more than just a good idea. You'll like him."

Violet had a hard time focusing on the conversation and pulling her mind off all her troubles. Meeting a new ministry partner was going to be hard, and who knew what Paul had told him about her. "So what did you tell him about me? Did you warn him that I got kidnapped the last time I was here?" Violet knew there was sarcasm in her voice and she immediately felt ashamed. "I'm sorry. That wasn't nice at all. Please forgive me."

"What happened to you, Violet? Why are you so bitter?"

Violet sighed. How could she even begin to explain? The weight of her secret was too heavy, but she didn't know if she could ever stop carrying it. The evidence of its destructive nature was everywhere, from her fractured relationships at home to the strained conversation she was having right now. But she had carried the secret for so long that the thought of sharing it seemed unthinkable, and her fear of what might happen after the secret was out left her helpless. Horrible things could happen, things like more kidnapping and even death! It just wasn't safe to let go of her secret. She was exhausted by it all, but there was no way out.

"Life... people... that's what's happened to me, Paul. But I'm truly sorry for how I've been acting today. Just because I've had a hard time with things, I have no excuse to be mean or ornery."

"All is forgiven. But maybe you should try a bit harder to be nice when you meet Everest..." Paul laughed. "He's just about as feisty as you and I wouldn't want you to be sent home!"

Violet looked at Paul to see if he was joking. Although he was grinning and the laugh lines around his eyes were more pronounced, there was an underlying seriousness to him. And why shouldn't there be? The last thing everyone needed was a volunteer stirring up trouble. And didn't she hope to stay here as a full-time worker? If so, she had better make sure she cleared her mind from all the turmoil in her life. Nothing was going to change the past, so she might as well work hard to make sure her past didn't change the direction she was going in the future.

"I'll try my hardest. I promise."

"That's all a person could ask for, Violet. Well, that and to pray for help and strength. Forgiveness is hard, but essential, Violet. You'll never recover from whatever secret you're hiding until you start forgiving people; the ones who kidnapped you... as well as yourself." As the late afternoon sun came streaming through the windshield, Paul pulled down the visor to shield his eyes from the glare. "This place isn't going to be an easy place to serve. I'd get my emotions in order if I were you. It's the only way you'll survive."

You can say that again. Violet knew she was going to be stretched beyond what she thought she could bear. She longed to be able to get her emotions in order like Paul suggested, but it was impossible. She may eventually be able to forgive herself, but she would never be able to forgive him. No, the memories of him and the things he had done to her were too vivid and painful.

As they drove past that awful street, Violet wondered just how much she could be stretched before she broke. Calle Escondido, also known as Hidden Street, looked just the same as the first time she had walked down it, and the memories it evoked seemed just as real as if she were living them again. With a sick feeling in her stomach, Violet thought about all the terrible secrets and memories that were tied up with that street. She could only hope they stayed hidden like the name suggested.

Chapter 7

November 1992

One shop led to the next until Violet found herself far from The Mission. Too far, actually, if she were to listen to the strict rules Pastor Paul had given her more than an hour earlier. "Stay close to The Mission and do not go anywhere near Calle Escondido. I know all the tourists talk about how great it is, but there's nothing worth buying there and it's not safe for you to go there alone." The words echoed in her mind as she stood just one block away from the very place he had told her not to go. Glancing up at the fading sun, Violet knew she should turn around and head back. Not only was she too far from The Mission, it was getting late. If she didn't hurry, it would be dusk before she returned to the safety of the old, three story building and the people inside.

Just as she was turning, she noticed that from where she stood she could hear the muffled noise of the shop owners calling out to the tourists as they passed by. Those voices blended with the sounds of a donkey braying, people laughing and cars honking. The very sounds coming from the street were enticing.

Knowing better, Violet took a few steps closer. Now she could see down the street and look at the things she wasn't supposed to see. Feeling as if her curiosity could be satisfied by simply looking from a distance, Violet took in the sights with glee. The noises she had heard only told half the story. Now she could see the other half. With animated gestures, the shop owners were waving various items for the tourists to see. She smiled as she watched the display between the two groups—the persistent salesmen and the tourists who wanted a good deal. Some of the people made purchases while others didn't. It was interesting to Violet to see the interaction and how determined the salesmen were; instead of defeat when being turned down, they simple honed in on the next tourist walking by.

The sound of a bray caught Violet's attention and she turned her head to look where the noise had originated. Surprised, she saw a donkey with a sombrero on its head. There was a ragged, brightly colored blanket on its back and the poor animal looked on in tired compliance as a little boy climbed onto the donkey for his parents to take a picture. Only after the couple paid the man who held the animal's reins, did Violet see the animal was painted to look like a zebra. The sight fueled her desire to walk that street. If there was a painted donkey, what else might there be?

Violet closed her eyes and scrunched her nose. A battle was raging within her—curiosity versus duty. She felt it was her job to obey the rules placed on her by Pastor Paul. That sense of duty resonated with her practical personality; there were things a person did in life simply because it was expected, it was the right thing to do. But there were times when her curious side seemed to speak louder than her practical side, and those times left Violet feeling vulnerable. While she argued back and forth with herself, ideas came up that she just couldn't deny. Why was it so wrong to walk this street? And what harm could really befall her in broad daylight? So what if all the things sold here were cheap tourist traps? She wasn't going to purchase anything anyway.

As she thought, her feet took tentative steps until she was standing on the sidewalk of Calle Escondido. She was at the end of the business section; walking to her right would lead her away from the shops, while walking to her left would take her into the heart of the hustle and bustle.

I've been practical all my life... Why not see this place? If I hurry, no one will ever know.

Turning to her left, Violet took a confident step. To anyone who may have been watching, the action was mundane and of little consequence. But for Violet, it represented a blow to the wall around her heart—the wall she had begun constructing the day her older sister had left the family to live with a boyfriend. Violet was only 12 years old at the time, but she had been mature enough to see how her beautiful sister had sought after the wrong things.

Instead of working hard for good grades during her high school years, Vivian had worked for attention from boys. Revealing clothing, too much make-up and a flirtatious personality were the tools Vivian had used to create the world she wanted. And once she started gaining the attention she so desperately desired, there was a fire lit within her that would only be satisfied by her ruin. The pain Vivian's choices had caused ran deep, not only in Vivian, but the whole family. Their shame, heartache and sadness only grew as news of Vivian would reach them. Each new snippet of information bearing more details of how sin and pleasure ruled the beautiful young woman, yet left her unhappy and unfulfilled.

The wall Violet had begun building grew higher and wider as choice by choice she swore she would not follow in her sister's footsteps. Violet chose modest clothing. She refused to wear make-up. She was open and friendly, but never flirtatious. She followed the rules and tried to be the best she could. Yet, those same desires that consumed her sister flared up in her own heart as well. And year after year, Violet feared the only thing keeping them at bay was the wall she had carefully built.

Each step Violet took toward the heart of Calle Escondido pounded at that wall. But with all the sights and sounds, Violet was unaware of the potential damage to her carefully constructed protection.

The first store she walked by had displays from floor to ceiling covered in bright purses. For a moment she was tempted to purchase one, but decided to keep walking.

There were so many things to look at and Violet meandered through many of the shops, enjoying the experience.

She had lost count of how many times people called out to her, and had grown accustomed to the flattery they used to get her to listen to them. "Pretty lady," "princess" and "beautiful" were the most common compliments, but they didn't work because Violet knew they weren't sincere.

As she stood on a street corner waiting to cross, a man with necklaces draped over his arm walked up to her. Without even asking, he took one of the long necklaces and put it over her head. The silver chain was beautiful and Violet was pleased by its beauty until the man started arranging it to lay flat on her chest. With swift hands, he pulled the long necklace down and out of her blonde hair. Then, even though the jewelry was perfectly placed, he continued to work with it, brushing the backs of his hands against her breasts. With a gasp, Violet pushed his hands away and pulled the necklace off.

"You no like, princess?" the man asked with a laugh. His dark, handsome face contradicted the ugliness Violet saw in his eyes. As he reached out to place a different necklace over her head, he said, "Try another?"

Feeling violated, Violet ducked her head to avoid his action and quickly walked away. Fear crept in as she looked up at the sky; the sun was setting faster than she had anticipated. Looking around, Violet noticed there was a different feel to the street now than when she had first came. There were fewer tourists and the ones who were still there looked less interested in the trinkets on display and more interested in the bars. The people milling around were smoking and drinking and there was a distinct harshness to them.

In her hurry to escape the man with the necklaces, Violet had gotten turned around and was uncertain which way she needed to go to get back to The Mission. Looking for street signs, she tried to locate the cross street that had brought her here in the first place. Pushing through the crowd while trying to find the signs was challenging and Violet tripped several times on the potholes riddling the street.

Stuffing back the panic that was growing at a rapid rate, Violet stopped walking. She needed to calm down and collect her thoughts instead of running around. She only knew one way to get back to The Mission, and if she didn't find the streets she knew, she was going to be lost. With a steadying sigh, Violet closed her eyes, shut her ears to the chaotic voices around her and whispered a prayer; a prayer of repentance for not listening to Pastor Paul and a prayer pleading for help.

When she opened her eyes, she thought for a moment that she was seeing an image of herself. If she were to embrace the desires she tried so hard to stifle, she would probably look just like the young woman standing before her. Almost identical in build and height, the girl's face was so similar that she could be mistaken for Violet's sister. She looked to be in her early 20's, but if the pound of make-up were washed off, she might look to be merely in her teens. Violet noticed her scant clothing, as well as the large man possessively holding her arm, and she wondered how the girl had ended up here and if she were happy. While Violet watched, the man let go of her and began fussing with her long brown hair. He said something to the girl, causing her to straighten her mini skirt and smooth the small sweater that barely covered her chest.

When the young woman looked over at Violet, her brown eyes seemed to mirror her own at first glance. They both had the same doe-like shade of brown, but there was sadness pooled in the girl's eyes, answering the question of whether she was happy or not. There was no denying the feelings those eyes evoked in Violet; she may not know the girl's story, but it was evident that she needed to be rescued. Pity swelled in her heart as she acknowledged how even though this girl may look like her, they were very different. Violet was free to leave this street and go home, but this girl was obviously trapped.

Suddenly, the man standing with the girl turned and looked right at Violet. A gleam lit his eye and he started walking toward her. Violet wasn't sure what the man intended, but she was sure to find out soon because her feet refused to move. Fear left her unable to flee from her quickly worsening situation.

Chapter 8

Violet jumped as a hand took her elbow. Tearing her eyes away from the piercing look of the girl and the menacing man walking toward her, Violet turned to see who dared to touch her. Without taking the time to see more than the fact that it was a young man who held her, she was frightened. She had half expected to see the man with the necklaces again.

"Excuse me! What do you think you are doing?" Violet's eyes blazed with anger and a growing amount of fear. "Let go of me!" She shouted as she tried to wrestle her arm free from his grip, but it was useless. His strength was far greater than hers.

"I'm sorry ma'am, but no." The words were spoken in fluent English and Violet paused in surprise. She had expected him to call her princess or pretty lady like all the other men who greeted her on this street. His dark complexion and hair had given the impression of a local, but his speech caused her to question her first impression.

"I won't let you go. Not until we are on our way back to The Mission. You're not safe here." Without waiting for Violet to respond, the man pulled her in the opposite direction from which she was going and started walking with confident steps. Violet had a hard time matching his quick strides and she wondered for a moment if he would just drag her if she refused to walk. But she had more important things to think about than whether she should be walking or not.

"How do you know where I work?" Violet demanded as they emerged from the busy street onto an abandoned side street. "Who are you? And why do you think it's your job to keep me safe? I was perfectly fine," she insisted. "I had everything under control." As the defiant words came out, she wondered who she was trying to convince. He seemed to doubt the claim, and the pounding of her heart declared she did as well.

The man stopped walking and let go of her arm. "My name is Santiago. I work in law enforcement. That's why I know you weren't safe. I know that street, and how it gets after dark."

When Violet simply nodded, he continued. "I happened to be walking by The Mission as you were leaving earlier today. I heard Pastor Paul tell you to be back before dark, so I assumed you are one of the volunteers."

Feeling a bit better about the situation, Violet allowed herself to smile a little. "Yes, I am a volunteer. And I'm going to be in big trouble if I'm not back there soon!"

Santiago nodded and grinned. "Well, allow me to escort you." With a flourish, he took a deep bow. Standing tall once again, he held out his hand as he laughed and said, "Walk this way, my lady."

Violet joined his laughter and allowed him to take her arm once again. This time, it was a gentle grasp and she was willing to let him lead. His calm demeanor, and the fact that he was in law enforcement, caused her to drop her defense. As her fear abated she felt a desire to trust him. "My name is Violet, by the way. Violet Thompson."

"What a beautiful name. I might say it's even more beautiful when spoken in Spanish... Violeta." The word flowed from his lips in a smooth, enticing way, leaving Violet with the feeling that she could listen to him talk to her in Spanish all day.

"I think just about anything sounds prettier in a language other than my own," Violet said as she looked around. She now recognized the streets and buildings surrounding her. It wouldn't be long until they reached The Mission.

"Possibly."

"So, how is it that you speak such fluent English?"

Santiago hesitated for a moment, and while she waited for him to respond, she noticed how thick his dark hair was and how evenly spaced his white teeth were. He looked to be around her age and she briefly wondered whether he was a Christian. After all, he knew Pastor Paul by name, and he was kind; goodness seemed to radiate from his dark eyes.

"I went to school in the States," he finally said.

"Were you raised here, or in the States?"

If he hadn't looked at her, Violet might have thought he hadn't heard her, for he seemed in no hurry to talk. They walked in silence for a few minutes and Violet enjoyed the companionable silence. She was so relieved that her almost unfortunate outing today had come to a pleasant ending. Walking on the arm of a handsome, well-built man who made her feel protected and safe was something she had only dreamt of. Maybe all those jokes her friend Rachel had made about finding Mr. Right in Mexico had some truth to them after all. Violet almost giggled as she remembered the teasing her friend had dished out while she helped Violet pack for the trip.

Violet didn't have long to ponder whether Santiago could truly be the sought after Mr. Right or not, because their walk had come to an end. Standing in front of The Mission now, Violet wished she could prolong their time together. Would she ever see him again? Would she ever get the chance to know if he believed in God?

"Hey, just so you know. What you did today was foolish." Santiago let go of her arm to reach up and tuck a stray piece of hair behind Violet's ear. "With such beautiful blonde hair, you are bound to attract a lot of attention, and not the kind of attention a girl like you wants. You shouldn't go anywhere near that section of town alone."

The words, *a girl like you*, reverberated in Violet's mind, mocking her. This man was a stranger, but he had assumed since she was a volunteer at The Mission that she wouldn't desire the kind of attention that could be found on

Calle Escondido. But he didn't know what lurked in her heart and mind.

Not certain of what to say, Violet simply shrugged and was relieved when Santiago spoke again. "Let me take you to see the sights around here. I know all the best places, and that way you can see everything while being safe."

"That would be nice of you."

"Believe me, the pleasure would be all mine." He once again bowed in a grand display of playful chivalry. "Until next time."

Santiago remained on the sidewalk until Violet entered The Mission and closed the door behind her. Peeking out the window, she watched him walk away. There was an element of mystery to this man and she found it intriguing. But there was also a feeling of safety. Spending more time with him was sure to be better than anything she could find on Calle Escondido.

As she prepared for bed that night, she contemplated seeking out Pastor Paul and asking him to forgive her for disobeying his instructions. Had it not been for Santiago, there was no telling what might have happened. But just as quickly as the idea came into her mind, so did her pride. It would be awfully humbling to admit she had knowingly defied the rules. Maybe if she asked God to forgive her and promised to never do it again, she could skip talking to Pastor Paul. Surely, what he didn't know wouldn't hurt him, and keeping this secret wouldn't hurt her either.

Chapter 9

April 1994

"Violet, this is Everest Marks. Everest, this is Violet Thompson." Pastor Paul smiled slightly as he looked from Violet to the young man he had just introduced as Everest. For some reason, when Paul told her about him, she had thought the name Everest would have belonged to an older person. The fact that he was probably close to her age surprised her.

Pastor Paul steadied his gaze on Everest and said, "She's the volunteer we were expecting next month."

"Yes, I remember you mentioning her expected arrival." Everest spoke first to Paul before turning to look at Violet. The action annoyed her and left her feeling as if the two men shared some secret concerning her. She was even more annoyed by the feelings of attraction Everest stirred in her. Being around attractive young men was unsettling, she felt vulnerable and self-conscious. With all the other reasons for not wanting to be at this new ministry, the last thing she needed was to work with someone who made her ill at ease.

Trying to be discreet in her quick evaluation of him, Violet noted how it wasn't so much that Everest was good looking, really; no, he was definitely average in that department. But there was something about the way he stood with confidence, the way he seemed to be in charge. And his broad shoulders were enough to make any woman feel feminine and petite in comparison. *But so were Shawn's.*

With that thought, Violet's throat tightened. The knowledge that Shawn was no longer her fiancé hit her with a force that came close to shattering the last small piece of her broken heart. She may be attracted to Everest, but she still longed for Shawn. Could she ever learn to love someone else?

"It's nice to meet you, Violet." Everest spoke and the sound of his voice brought Violet's mind back from her sorrowful thoughts. He held out his huge hand and Violet responded by placing hers in it. Shaking her hand, Everest looked into her eyes and grinned. "Paul has told me all about how dedicated you are and how hard you work. He has nothing but good things to say about you."

Immediately, Violet felt ashamed. Of course Pastor Paul hadn't gossiped about her. She glanced in his direction and caught him looking at her. His eyes seemed to be saying, "I told you so."

How have I become so jaded by life that I would doubt the character of kindhearted Pastor Paul?

Deep down, Violet knew she needed to work on forgiveness. Paul was right. It was impossible to think she could minister to people while carrying around such baggage; because of that baggage, her thoughts had turned cynical and judgmental. But who could blame her? Not only had she been kidnapped the last time she was here, she had arrived home from Mexico just in time to help her beloved friend when a seemingly harmless neighbor turned psychotic and began stalking her. No doubt the ordeal had been hardest on Rachel, but it had scarred Violet as well. A person just never knew who they could trust anymore.

Even so, the landscape of her heart had been altered too much, and she admitted to herself that she had allowed the evil people in the world to affect how she viewed the good people.

"All I can say is I hope you're not disappointed." Violet looked down at her feet as she responded to Everest's kind greeting. She couldn't bear to return his direct gaze. He may think her action was one of humility, but it wasn't. It was one of shame.

"I'm sure I won't be disappointed in the least."

His comment gave her courage to look up at him, and as she looked into his sincere hazel eyes, she hoped with every fiber of her being he was right.

* ● ● ◉ ◎ ● ●

The next few days opened Violet's eyes to just how wrong she had been. Her time at the soup kitchen had been pleasant and Everest had proved to be a wonderful ministry partner. His simple, down-to-earth attitude towards life had calmed the jumbling emotions in Violet's heart and mind. Although nothing had been resolved concerning her relationships back home or her hidden past here, she felt less troubled and more confident that eventually it would all work out.

Even though she had only been back in Mexico for a few days, she had already been out in the town to do some shopping. Her hurried trip to the mall had provided her with most of the things she needed to replace her lost luggage, but now that she was here in Mexico, she realized she had forgotten to purchase socks. It had been a quick walk to town and back, but she had enjoyed being out in the sunshine and soaking up the culture around her as she went to her favorite stores.

Even though she wasn't at The Mission, the Mesa Vecindad was still within walking distance from all the stores she had shopped at the first time she was here. The familiarity of those places was welcome; and her shopping didn't take long because she already knew where to find things. However, she was very careful to avoid certain places. Not all the familiar places were ones she wished to visit.

While she was at her favorite jewelry store, she picked up a beautiful jeweled brooch for Nana Rosa. The elderly woman lived at the soup kitchen, providing a proper chaperone for Everest the past few months he had been working at the house and now, for Violet as well. Violet didn't know the woman very well because she mostly stayed in her room resting or reading, but she wanted to show a kindness to her for the warm welcome she had given Violet. The woman had demanded Violet call her Nana Rosa like all the other people she loved even though they had just met. Calling her Nana Rosa instead of something more formal was hard at first, but the woman insisted she would rather be called Nana than anything else.

Since her arrival, Everest had kept her busy with many different tasks. Because the idea of opening Mesa Vecindad was somewhat new, there were many details to work out. Simple yet time consuming jobs like sorting food supplies, clothing, and toiletries were just some of the things that needed Violet's attention. Many churches in the States had sent boxes of those items and Violet had spent countless hours organizing their generous gifts.

The task before her today was mending. While the majority of the clothing that had been donated was in good shape, some of them were missing buttons or had small tears. Upon seeing the pile that needed mending, Everest had laughed and said it was a good thing Violet was there since he would have just thrown the items away. She doubted the truth of the statement; he probably would have taken them to Anna, but it felt good to be needed. And with a needle in one hand and thread in the other, she set out to show Everest just how important her role in this new ministry could be. A determined look crossed her face, followed by a smile. Not only would she work hard to show Everest her importance, she would show Shawn, Rachel, and her parents just how wrong they were when they questioned her decision to come here.

As her needle deftly placed buttons, the stress Violet had been carrying seemed to melt away. For as long as she could remember, her mother had said there was nothing more soothing to the soul than mending. "It's a good reminder of how God can take the torn fabric of our lives and make it whole again," she would always say. Violet could almost hear her now, "Psalm 147, Verse 3 tells us that God 'heals the brokenhearted and binds up their wounds.' Sweet girl, don't you ever forget that. There will come a day when you will need to remember that promise. And when you do, let God stitch your heart back together."

It didn't matter how many times Violet had heard her mother say those words; they still impacted her as if she had heard them for the first time. And now, even though she was miles and miles away from her, Cora was still imparting wisdom to her daughter.

Praying while she stitched the clothing in her hands, Violet felt connected to God. It was the closest He had felt since she had left the States. Maybe her stubborn heart was finally still enough to listen. Maybe she was finally allowing God to work His needle and thread through her broken heart.

A brief flicker of a memory flashed through her mind; a memory of her sister, Vivian, walking out the front door of their childhood home all those years ago. Did Vivian ever think of Mom? Did she hear Cora's words repeating wisdom in her heart like Violet did?

Violet was so intent on her work and her thoughts, she didn't hear the knock on the front door.

"No need to get up... I'm just all the way in the back room, but I can get it!" Everest teased Violet as he walked past her to answer the door. His sense of humor had erased all of the feelings of discomfort she had felt upon meeting him. She may still be attracted to him, but he made her laugh so much she had forgotten to feel self-conscious.

Violet giggled before she returned her focus to the needle in her hand. She just had a tiny bit more to sew and she would be done with the long, flowing skirt she was working on.

Barely paying attention to the voices at the front door, Violet was surprised when Everest ushered someone into the kitchen. Standing before her was a woman holding a vase with a single red rose in it. She wore a black apron embroidered with brilliant orange words that Violet assumed advertised a floral shop. With a shy smile, the woman looked at Everest.

When he nodded and grinned, she turned to Violet and said, "Miss Violet?"

"Yes, I'm Violet."

"For you," the woman said as she held out the vase. When Violet took it from her hands, she nodded and hurriedly turned to walk away.

"Gracias!" Violet called to the woman before she closed the door.

"I'm shocked! You do speak Spanish," Everest laughed. Days ago, when he had found out about Violet's inability to speak the nation's language, he had teased her ruthlessly. And though he continued to tease her, he had also promised to help her learn.

"Oh, whatever!" Violet rolled her eyes. Holding the bloom to her nose, she smelled its sweet fragrance. "I wonder who this could be from?"

"Well, there's an envelope. Open it."

As Violet opened the envelope, Everest smiled and walked away. She thought the action odd and wondered why he wasn't curious about who sent the rose. Pulling out the tiny card, she was relieved to see the note was written in English. The meticulous handwriting was easy to read.

Something beautiful for someone beautiful.

The words instantly brought a smile to her face. What a sweet gesture. But who sent it?

Hearing Everest humming an old hymn in the next room as he worked, Violet began to wonder. Was it possible that Everest had sent her the gorgeous red rose?

Chapter 10

Though her sleeves were rolled up, Violet was still overly warm. The thick apron she wore may have provided protection against spills, but she was seriously contemplating taking it off. Heat radiated from the stove top where she was cooking a large pot of beans. She had several chickens roasting in the oven and a stack of tortillas keeping warm in a towel on the table. It was simple fare, but with the right seasonings, it would be delicious. Stepping back with a contented sigh, Violet acknowledged that working at the soup kitchen was indeed a good fit for her. For years, cooking had been a passion for her. When her mom taught her to make cookies at the age of nine, Violet had discovered the joy of mixing ingredients to make something delicious. Her mother had encouraged her to explore the culinary world, and as a result, Violet had become an excellent cook.

After checking the beans and the roasting meat, Violet walked over to the shelving that held the dishes. She picked up four ceramic plates and walked over to the table. A smile crossed her face as she moved the red rose that had been delivered earlier that day to the center of the table. Curiosity about who sent it invaded her mind, distracting her for a minute. But when she heard footsteps in the hall, she quickly resumed her task of setting the table.

Each day, Violet would fix a large amount of food for the noon meal. It was the only meal they provided for the people who sought their help. Mesa Vecindad was open from late morning to early afternoon during the week, but closed on the weekends and evenings. So, every night it was just Everest and Nana Rosa who joined Violet at the dinner table. Tonight, however, Pastor Paul was to join them.

"¿Violeta? ¿Como estás?" Nana Rosa said in her soft voice as she entered the room. The old woman shuffled her feet more than she actually walked. She was slightly stooped with age, and at times her wrinkled hands shook with the first stages of palsy. But whatever physical ailments she had, she more than made up for them with her enjoyable, quick wit. Even though Rosa and Violet knew very little of each other's language, they communicated incredibly well and Violet had quickly learned that Rosa missed nothing. Even the slightest sigh or weary yawn would result in a caring, grandmotherly comment.

"I'm almost finished with dinner, Nana Rosa," Violet said as she pulled out a chair and motioned for Rosa to take a seat. With a smile of satisfaction, Violet saw the green, sparkly brooch pinned to the woman's shawl. It amazed her that the woman would feel the need for a shawl in this hot kitchen, but it pleased her nonetheless to see that Rosa wore the pin.

Violet was given a smile and a kiss on the forehead before Rosa sank into the hard wooden chair. Violet made sure Rosa was comfortable before turning back to the stove. Then, with deft movements, she quickly filled a large bowl with beans and placed them on the table. She had just removed the chickens from the oven when Everest, followed by Paul, walked into the spacious kitchen.

"Come on in, it's okay," Paul said, looking behind him at someone who was hidden behind the doorway. He reached out his hand and Violet watched with curiosity as a tall, willowy girl emerged through the door, holding onto Paul's hand with a ferocious grip.

With guarded eyes, the girl began to look around the room. She held the attention of everyone as they were all a little uncertain as to what they should do next.

Paul cleared his throat and said, "Everyone, this is Mariela, she... " Before he could finish the introduction, the girl saw Violet. Dropping Paul's hand, she ran to her, wrapped Violet in a crushing hug, and sobbed.

Feeling overwhelmed, Violet looked to Pastor Paul as she made soothing noises to the hysterical girl in her arms. "Do you speak English, sweetie?" Violet asked Mariela. The girl didn't even act as if she had heard Violet's question. Violet looked at Paul and when he shook his head no, she sighed, feeling helpless.

In between her sobs, the girl was saying the same sentence over and over. Even if it wasn't spoken in Spanish,

Violet doubted if she would have been able to understand the girl because she was crying so hard.

With slow, deliberate movements, Rosa scooted her chair back from the table and stood. She shuffled over to where the two girls were still locked in a tight embrace. Placing her shaking hands on the girls head, Rosa began to pray out loud.

In a voice shaking with emotion, Violet began to pray as well.

Soon, Paul and Everest had joined the circle and added their prayers to the confusion. It was a moment that would change Violet forever. Even though she prayed while trying to soothe the girl in her arms, she was keenly aware of the situation. One young woman, obviously upset, was surrounded by four people who genuinely cared. This was what the kingdom of God was supposed to look like—a place for people to run to when they were hurting.

When the girl was finally calm, everyone took a seat at the table. Violet had quickly finished dishing up the food while Everest put another plate and fork on the table. Paul led the group in a prayer of thanks for the food and everyone began filling their plates, eager to satisfy their hunger. The mundane actions of dinnertime offered a blessed break from the intensity of the moments before.

Suddenly, Mariela stood up and asked Paul a question. Violet recognized enough of the words to know she was asking where the bathroom was. With curiosity, she watched the young woman leave the room, then turned to Paul.

"Why was she so upset?" Violet asked him.

The man looked at her with eyes that were filled with his own unspoken questions; pressing his lips into a firm line, he seemed to be choosing his words carefully. He sighed, and then turned to look at Everest. Violet was reminded of the glance the men had shared upon her meeting Everest and she was again annoyed that they seemed to share information she didn't have.

Everest shrugged his shoulders and raised his eyebrows the slightest bit, looking at a loss. Then Paul leveled his gaze on Violet again. With a sigh he said, "The girl claimed to know you. She said her sister worked the streets with you."

Chapter 11

Guilt flooded Violet's body and gathered in her ears, turning them crimson. Although she didn't remember meeting the girl, Violet knew it was possible that she had indeed recognized her.

Both Paul and Everest were staring at her, waiting for a response. But Violet wasn't sure what she should say. How much of the truth did they really need to know? And how much could they know without having serious problems?

"I uh… I certainly have never worked the streets!" Violet declared, knowing full well the statement would only alleviate some of their curiosity, but not all.

Suspicion filled Everest's eyes. "Of course you haven't, but why does she say she knows you?"

"That's what I am wondering…" Paul agreed. "And why does she say she knew you had been kidnapped and has worried about you ever since?"

"Wait…she knows that?"

"That's what she claims." Paul reached out and took Violet's hand. "Are you sure you don't know her?"

Paul's fatherly gesture was just about her undoing. Tears rushed to her eyes and her throat closed around a lump so large she could barely swallow. Was it really just a few hours earlier that she had felt certain all her problems would be resolved?

Closing her eyes, Violet allowed her mind to take her back to the day she had been kidnapped. Everything had happened so quickly. She honestly didn't remember as much about the day as she thought she would, and for that she was grateful. But as she slowly replayed the chain of events, she realized Mariela had indeed been there. The knowledge stunned her and shook her to the core all at the same time. If the girl had been there, how much did she really know?

"I think... I, well..." Violet struggled to answer. "I think she must be confused."

The lie slipped through her lips and Violet was shamed by the lack of guilt she felt. She hadn't kept her secret hidden this long to just start telling everything the first time someone came forward with a piece of truth. Besides, right now, she wasn't even certain the girl knew the whole story. And if she didn't, Violet was much better off keeping quiet. No, she couldn't tell them she remembered the girl; it was much smarter to simply wait and see what would happen.

Thankfully, her lie seemed to satisfy the men. They both began eating and soon the conversation shifted to another subject. The young woman in question returned to the table, appearing to be content to simply eat and stare at Violet. It was unnerving to be stared at, but Violet tried to ignore the feelings of panic that grew at a rapid rate. How long was the girl going to stay here?

She had just decided to ask Paul to help her talk to the girl when he spoke. "Thank you Violet, for a wonderful meal." He scooted his chair back and stood. "It's getting late and I need to get Mariela home. She just moved into The Mission today and has experienced a lot recently. She was abandoned by her parents when they left for the States and thankfully she knew to come to us. Praise the Lord she won't have to follow in her sister's footsteps and work the streets!"

Breathing a sigh of relief, Violet bid the girl goodbye. As Mariela stepped out the door, Violet turned to say goodbye to Paul. Instead of simply waving goodbye like he normally would, Paul pulled Violet into a hug.

"I will talk to you later," he whispered in her ear. Then, he let go. He looked her in the eyes, communicating a silent message, and then turned to wave at Everest. Violet breathed a little easier when the door closed behind him.

Feeling wary about Everest and his suspicious gaze, Violet turned from watching Paul and Mariela to face the awkwardness head-on. *Might as well get it over with.*

But instead of asking her questions, Everest simply said goodnight and walked away. *What a strange man. Does he not have a curious bone in his body?*

· ∘ ◎●◐ ∘ ·

"Let me reward your hard work with the best tacos you have ever eaten!" Everest's eyes were sparkling in boyish delight.

It had taken all day for Violet to get over the conversation from the night before. The nightmares she had suffered through the night were strange combinations of truth and fiction, and they all included the hysterical girl who claimed to know Violet. The disturbing dreams had bothered her greatly and the only way Violet knew to combat those memories was to pour herself completely into her work. As a result, all the sorting, mending and organizing had been accomplished, along with serving the noon meal. Everest had been very impressed, and honestly, Violet was, too.

"That sounds great!" Violet responded with just as much enthusiasm as he showed. "But the best I've ever eaten? Are you sure?"

"How dare you question my judgment?"

Violet punched him in the arm and then ran a few steps from the kitchen into the great room to avoid retaliation. When he followed, Violet began to tease him. "How could I not question it? Just look at your hair? You certainly haven't used good judgment in deciding to let it get so long… " She took her hands and held them a few inches from the top of her head. "The result is… ah… bushy?"

Laughing, Everest ran toward Violet. When she ducked out of his reach again, he pretended she was too quick and agile for him to catch. However, one stride from his long legs would have been more than enough to put her in his reach. "Hey! How dare you mock my hair! I just thought I would make my hair match my name. You know, give myself a wild 'mountain man' look."

"Mountain man? You can't be serious!" Violet rolled her eyes. "Now, if you said you were trying to look like Sasquatch, well, then I would have to say you succeeded."

"Sasquatch!" Everest exclaimed as he lowered his brows in a pretend glare. "Now you've done it. Just for that, no tacos for you!"

Violet instantly quit laughing and reached out to grab his arm. "No! Please, forgive me. I must have those tacos!" She worked hard to come across as serious, but laughter bubbled out after her last words.

"You are forgiven. But only because I'm hungry." He picked up Violet's sweater from the back of the chair and held it out to her. Violet took it from his hands and allowed him to usher her out the door. "Seriously though, should I get a haircut?"

* ∘ ◦ ⬤ ◦ ∘ *

"I would ask you why you are here, but since you are a woman who likes to keep her information to herself I assume it's no use." Everest had polished off four tacos and was ready to begin chatting. Violet, however, was still in the middle of her second. She was amazed at how fast he ate. And frustrated by his statement. He didn't understand that she had a valid reason for not sharing everything. *But he's just met me; how could he understand?*

"Well, would it surprise you if I answered your non-question?"

"Actually, it would." He dropped his eyes to look at the napkin next to his plate. He seemed nervous and Violet wondered if he was finally going to begin asking her about how Mariela fit into her past.

"I'm here, right now, eating the best tacos I've ever eaten because I lost everything worth staying for back home."

Everest looked up from the napkin, "Tell me about it."

He was challenging her to open up, to tell him something personal. Telling him about Shawn wasn't nearly as big a deal as telling him about her last trip to Mexico. And so, she took the challenge and told him all about Shawn; how she had loved him and how he had broken her heart.

"You know I wasn't supposed to be here yet. But, when Shawn and I broke up... " Tears welled in Violet's brown eyes. "Well, I guess I just wanted to run away from the pain."

Everest looked at her with serious eyes. The moment was intense, too intense, and Violet felt uncomfortable by the emotion she saw expressed in his face.

To lighten the mood, she said, "Isn't that what criminals do? Flee the country?"

As the joke left her mouth, she realized that it wasn't funny. *Isn't that exactly what Shawn had said? Didn't he think Frank Smith had fled to Mexico? To this very city?*

"So, you're telling me you're a criminal?" The question was asked without a hint of a smile. And Everest looked almost angry.

Violet gasped. Her eyes grew round and she didn't know what to say. She knew he was aware that she had some secrets, but did he really think her a criminal? "Of course, I'm not!"

Her indignant response broke through Everest's façade. Laughter spilled from his smiling face and then he said, "I really had you going for a minute!"

"You're too much. You know that?" The humor was lost on Violet and all she felt was anger. Was there ever a serious thought in that man's brain?

Suddenly all the mirth left his demeanor and he leaned forward. "But what if I were to tell you that I am the criminal who fled to Mexico?"

His whispered question sent chills up Violet's spine. "Come on Everest, that's not funny."

"No, it's not." Defeat saturated his words. "The truth rarely is."

Violet couldn't form a reply. How could he switch gears so quickly? She didn't know if she should laugh or be scared. How was it possible that this caring, generous man was a criminal? For lack of knowing what to do, Violet picked at the food on her plate with her fork. She no longer had an appetite. His silence confirmed that Everest was no longer joking, he was actually being serious.

As the shock from his statement wore off, curiosity set in. "So, what did you do?"

"I didn't do anything." He let out a weary sigh and Violet's heart squeezed in sympathy. "I was accused and convicted of fraud."

"What?" Although Violet had no idea what she had thought had happened, this wasn't at all what she had expected.

"Yeah. It's a long, complicated story."

"I've got time."

Everest looked at her for a moment as if deciding whether to tell her or not. Then, as if he was in a hurry to get it over with, he starting talking so fast Violet could barely keep up. "I was dating a woman who attended the church where I was pastoring. After we had been dating for a few months, she came to me and told me about a mission she used to volunteer at. She told me wonderful stories of how this tiny church in Nigeria was impacting their community and how God was doing amazing things. She said she was in close contact with the wife of the pastor there and they had recently told her they were going to lose their church building."

Everest laughed a bitter laugh and shook his head. "Fool that I am, I believed her and asked what I could do to help."

"Everest! You're not a fool!" Violet interrupted him.

"Of course I am. I fell right into her trap. Our church had recently been the benefactor of a large sum of money, money that was given with no expectations or instructions how to use it. She knew that and so she talked me into asking the financial team if they would agree to give the money to the mission. They agreed and then we took it before the church. Everyone got so excited at the prospect of helping that no one batted an eye when she asked for monthly donations as well."

"Wait, didn't the money go through a missionary organization or something? How did this woman end up with the money?"

"It was this huge thing. She was just one person who worked for a 'business' that had a fake ministry. Churches all over the United States were targeted. But when they all started reporting the scam instead of handing them money like we did, the truth came out. And when it did, the whole church was so distressed, they blamed me. It's a long, exhausting story, but I was tried and convicted as an accomplice."

Violet could not stop the tears in her eyes. What a horrible chain of events. "Oh, Everest."

"I took the punishment; I had no choice. But as soon as I was finished, I left the States. There was no sense trying to find another pastorate position; my name was forever ruined. I decided that if my life had been turned upside down in such a terrible way simply for the fact that I wanted to help a mission, why not actually go and work at one myself? But I think there was also a part of me that simply wanted to run from the pain. So… you and I," he smiled halfheartedly, "we aren't all that different I guess."

"No," Violet said as she reached out and took his hand. "We both have things in our past we wish we could forget."

Everest closed his eyes as a single tear fell from his eye. "And we both know what it feels like to be brokenhearted."

The emotion of the moment seemed to draw Violet and Everest together in a special bond, a bond created by mutual loss and hurt. And so, it came as no surprise when Everest expressed a desire to prolong their evening together.

But when he suggested watching the sunset at the beach, she'd had no idea which beach he meant. If she had, she might not have agreed to go. Sitting on the sand, watching the waves roll in while the sky turned brilliant shades of pink and red, memories began to roll in as well. The memories she'd made on that very beach were ones that she didn't want to remember. And as Everest chattered happily next to her, Violet seemed to drift away to another time, a time she wished she could change.

Chapter 12

December 1992

The sand between her toes was warm and the sun was shining down on her head, making her golden hair just as warm as the sand. It seemed impossible that it was December 1st.

Violet had finished up her work at The Mission for the day and had sought solace at the beach. Homesickness caused her to seek the sandy shores of her favorite beach every chance she got. While it wasn't nearly the same as the rock studded beaches back home, the roar of the waves and the soul soothing perspective could still be found here.

Things had been going well at The Mission and Violet's passion for missions had only deepened since her arrival. But there was a part of her that felt out of place in that world. Was she ready to leave her life in the States behind?

Was she ready to embrace this different life with abandon?

The weight of those questions seemed to pull her down, and with a sadness she didn't understand, she struggled to find the answers she needed.

"Mind if I join you?"

The question startled her and she jumped. Feeling foolish for being so easily scared, Violet laughed in embarrassment as she looked up to see who had spoken.

"Santiago!" Violet couldn't help the smile that spread across her face. A few days ago, Violet had taken him up on his offer to show her around the town. He had been an excellent tour guide, just like he had promised, and Violet now felt satisfied that she had seen all the places this city had to offer.

"Please, sit!" Violet patted the vacant half of the beach towel she was sitting on. "I guess it looks like I was expecting someone to come share this with me!"

Santiago sat and then looked into her eyes, "Maybe your heart was expecting me and just didn't know it…"

The comment sent a thrill of delight down her spine. *He's so romantic!*

Santiago took off his shoes and stretched his long legs out in front of him. "So, Violeta, tell me about your day. Surely you've not strayed too far from The Mission alone this time?"

Violet smiled as she shook her head no, reassuring him that she had been smarter than to make the same mistake twice. "Well, there's really not that much to tell about my day. Things are going really well for me at The Mission, and I was just sitting here thinking about whether I wanted to stay here full-time or if I want to pursue something else with my life."

"Such deep thoughts for such a pretty day. But if you ask me, I say..." He reached down and grasped her hand, raising it to his lips for a series of gentle kisses. "Stay."

His lips felt hot on her fingers. And their heat seemed to ignite the burning embers in her heart, embers she had tried so desperately to put out. But no matter how hard she tried, the passions that reminded her so much of her sister refused to be extinguished.

Turning to look up at the man who kissed her hand, Violet couldn't help but question her desire to be free from what was burning in her heart. *Wouldn't passion be a good thing if I loved the man? If Santiago is indeed "Mr. Right" and we get married, wouldn't God want me to desire him? I'm certain He would.*

Those thoughts nestled into Violet's mind and started to change the way she thought about herself. Maybe she didn't need to try so hard to deny those desires; maybe she just needed to be careful about who she felt those things for. In her quest to know what God wanted for that part of her life, she had read Song of Solomon, and the things she read there certainly didn't lack passion.

Feeling vulnerable, Violet smiled and said, "So what about you? Does that mean you want to stay here, too? Does your work keep you here?"

At the mention of work, Santiago's whole body tightened. And with a tired, weary sigh he said, "I don't want to talk about work. I want to talk about you and how beautiful you are."

"You're too much, you know that?" Violet scolded him, but she didn't mean it.

The silence that was so normal in their relationship settled over them once again. Santiago was content to simply look at her and she blushed beneath his gaze. For lack of knowing what else to do, Violet turned to watch the waves, and Santiago followed her lead.

"What are your dreams?" Santiago asked the question while he gazed at the ocean. A part of him seemed miles away. "What drives you to get out of bed each morning?"

The change of topic surprised Violet. Taking a moment to think about her answer, she scrunched her toes and felt the tickle of sand stuck between them. "What drives me out of bed is the thought of being a better person than I was the day before. And not just better… I want to be someone who helps people. I want to reach the people who feel hopeless and offer them hope. God's hope."

Santiago inhaled sharply and closed his eyes. He set his jaw and for a moment, Violet would have sworn he was fighting back tears, but then he spoke and Violet thought maybe it was anger he fought. "Doesn't it seem pointless sometimes?"

The question rendered Violet speechless. By looking at the man, she would say he struggled with some sort of personal defeat or loss. But the bitterness in his voice made her wonder if maybe he had been witness to someone else's loss while feeling unable to help.

Santiago still held her hand firmly in his grip and she squeezed it, "Striving to be better or to help people is never pointless."

When he turned to look at her, she had expected him to say something that fit within the current topic, but instead he said, "Let's go."

As he stood, he let go of her hand. And Violet felt saddened by the loss of his touch. "Go where?" she asked.

"I'm taking you home. But first, I need to walk through Calle Escondido."

"Wait, I'm not going back there. That street was awful. You said it yourself that I don't belong there. And the sun is almost set." Violet took small steps away from Santiago, as if putting distance between them would take away the feelings of fear that pounded in her heart. "Please, take me home another way?"

"Violeta." Santiago walked toward her and reached out his hand. "Don't you trust me? I would never put you in harm's way! I'm in law enforcement, remember?"

"I remember that, but why do you have to take me there? Why can't you go after you take me home?"

"Because I am not expected to be on that street right now. And that is the best time to see what is really happening. I promise you, I will not let you get hurt. Do you trust me?"

Violet placed a tentative hand in the one he held out. "I trust you."

Chapter 13

Walking down Calle Escondido was definitely different this time. Not only was Violet prepared for the sights and sounds, she was on the arm of a man. A strong, good looking man whose physical appearance caused him to fit in with the crowd.

What was not different, however, was the attention she got. The catcalls and remarks were just as persistent and scandalous. Feeling uncertain as to how Santiago felt about the attention she was receiving, Violet looked up to see his face. What she saw surprised her. Instead of the jealousy she had anticipated, Santiago's face showed only pride. Was it possible that Santiago took pride in her appearance?

She knew she shouldn't let it, but a measure of giddiness rose up within her. *So this is what it feels like to be found attractive...*

As they walked, Violet's hand firmly on Santiago's strong arm, she marveled at how secure she felt. He made her feel safe and she liked that. Santiago was scanning the street with determination and she wondered what he was looking for.

Passing several clusters of men who surrounded the girls who worked the street, Violet was reminded of the first time she saw them. Shaking her head the tiniest bit, she remembered how she had wondered if those girls liked the attention they got. The idea of being admired, even if for only one reason, had struck a chord of longing in her heart. But now, on the arm of a man who cared for her for more reasons than what she could do for him, Violet knew the women couldn't possibly be happy. Surely they longed for more, surely they longed for a way to escape.

When those thoughts entered Violet's mind, Santiago paused. Feelings of being caught caused her pulse to speed. But he couldn't possibly know the thoughts swirling in her mind, could he? When she dared to look at him, it was obvious that he wasn't paying attention to her at all. Something had caught his eye from across the street and he was so intent on whatever it was, Violet began searching the faces to see if she could make sense of his determined stare.

A gasp escaped her lips. There she was. The girl from the last time she was here. But something was different about her. Carefully looking the girl up and down, Violet decided it was her hair. The long blonde curls hung prettily around the girls shoulders. *Maybe it's not her... I would have sworn she had dark hair.*

Santiago muttered something under his breath and Violet turned, maybe he was talking to her. But he wasn't, he was still completely absorbed in whatever he was looking at across the street. Since she didn't need to respond to whatever Santiago had muttered, she turned back to the girl to get a better look. She wanted to see if it was indeed the same person she had seen before.

The moment Violet turned her attention back to her, the girl turned to look at her as well. The same sad, brown eyes looked at her, and Violet was certain it was indeed the young woman who had made such an impression on her before.

With her eyes pleading for Violet's help, the girl put her hand in her pocket and pulled out a folded piece of paper. Discreetly showing it to Violet, she mouthed the words "help me." The girl glanced at the men around her and then, when they weren't looking, she dropped the paper. As the paper slipped from her hand, she nodded toward it while she held eye contact with Violet, and then walked away from it.

The interchange left Violet with the chills. She needed to get that note. Thinking quickly, she squeezed Santiago's arm. "Oh, let's go over there. I want to see that suitcase! It's so old and has so much charm!"

Still distracted, Santiago acknowledged her request by simply letting her pull him where she wanted to go. As she walked toward the shop, she went right past the girl. Just when she was where the note lay on the ground, Violet purposely dropped her purse.

"Oh, no!" she cried as she knelt down to pick up her items. Santiago knelt as well and offered to help, but Violet waved him off as she slipped the note into her purse. In no time at all, Violet was once again walking toward the shop that displayed the old suitcase.

Minutes later, Violet was walking back to The Mission with an old, brown and yellow striped suitcase in her right hand while her left hand was holding onto Santiago's arm. Her curiosity about whatever had caused him to be so focused back on Calle Escondido was forgotten, the only thing she could think about was the note tucked safely in her purse.

The whole time they walked, Santiago seemed to be miles away. Violet decided that he must be thinking about something serious because there was a crinkle in his brow and his lips were set in a firm line.

When they arrived at The Mission, Santiago seemed to come out of his haze and he looked at her with tenderness in his eyes. "How did I come to be so blessed? A beautiful woman — whose beauty shines without make-up or revealing clothing — has allowed me to walk with her on my arm today."

The comment about make-up puzzled her. Uncertain what to make of the comment and how to respond, Violet simply looked at him and smiled a shy smile.

Before she even knew what was happening, he leaned closer to her. Wrapping his right arm around her waist, he pulled her close as he caressed her face with his left hand. "Life is bearable simply because you are in it." He whispered the words against her lips. Then he kissed her, full on the lips.

Completely taken off guard, Violet felt panic tingle up her body. Half of her wanted to escape the intoxicating feel of his lips on hers, while the other part thrilled. This may not be how she had envisioned her first kiss, but it was romantic and exciting just the same.

When his lips left hers, he promised to see her again and then he walked away, leaving Violet standing there breathless.

Chapter 14

With shaking hands, Violet opened the note. She wasn't sure what she was going to find as she unfolded the crumpled paper, but the memory of those brown eyes haunted her. By opening the note, she was probably placing herself in danger because after seeing her silent pleading, Violet knew she would do just about anything to help the girl.

Inhaling deeply to steady herself, Violet began to read the hastily written words.

Meet me at Playa Del Sol. At the bench behind the jewelry store. 10 am tomorrow. Please!

The request would require a lot of work on Violet's part. Most of her responsibilities had her hard at work until later in the day.

The whole time she went through her nightly routine, her mind worked the problem. She would make it happen, she would be there.

As she crawled into her bed, sleep was a million miles away. Between Santiago's kiss and the nameless girl's note, Violet felt as if she could easily think all night.

· ◦ ●◉● ◦ ·

The wind was unusually strong, and as Violet sat on the old bench behind the jewelry store, she wished she would have taken the time to tie her hair back before she had come. The minutes crawled by, allowing Violet to replay the conversation she'd had with Paul. It bothered her that she had lied to him, but what else could she have done? She had to have a reason to leave The Mission at such a crucial time in the day, and none of the reasons she could come up with were the truth. Blazing hot shame scorched its way across her heart. Not only had she hidden her excursion onto Calle Escondido, now she was blatantly lying.

Her moments of guilt were brought to an end when a small woman, with a brightly colored green and gold scarf draped around her head, took a seat on the bench next to her.

"You came." Relief flooded her whispered words.

"I did."

Pulling back the scarf, the girl looked at Violet. She was young, probably no older than twenty. And even though she had the reputation she did, there was an innocence, a vulnerability to her that Violet could not deny.

"My name is Violet; what's yours?"

"Misty," she said as tears flooded her eyes. "But that's not what the men call me. They refuse to use my real name because they refuse to see that I am a real person."

Violet felt at a loss. What was she to say?

"I don't have much time. You have to do something... you have to help me..." Misty looked at the various people walking by. She was scared. "You have to get me back to the States, I don't belong here. I'm a U.S. citizen."

"How long have you been here? How come no one has come looking for you?" Violet felt heartbroken and helpless.

"I've been here long enough to know that I am..." Misty began to cry. Her voice broke, but she forced the next word out, "pregnant."

Violet had to swallow to keep her own tears back. "Does anyone know?"

"No, and that's why I am with you right now. I have to get away. I have to keep this baby. I know my pimp will make me abort it. But this baby, I need it. I don't care who the father is..." Misty put her hand over her mouth to stop the sobs. But it didn't work.

"No, no, it doesn't matter who fathered it, this baby inside you is precious!" Violet reached out and rubbed the girl's back. "Can I contact your family for you? They can come get you."

"You don't understand! I have no family!" Misty angrily wiped at the tears on her face. "I was abandoned by my parents, and then I was abandoned by my foster parents. Taylor is the only person who ever loved me and now he's gone, too! But the baby, I don't know, but the baby might be his."

Violet reached into her purse and pulled out a tissue. Handing it to Misty she asked, "Who is Taylor?"

Misty wiped her eyes with a shaking hand. "Taylor was in the same foster home as me. They were good people, but when Taylor turned eighteen they told him he couldn't live there anymore. We were both so hurt that we decided it was the world against us. So we got married and came here for our honeymoon... and we were so happy, but... that's when..." Misty's lips trembled as she tried to tamp down her emotions. Unable to control the tears, she covered her face with her hands and wept. Her sobs ripped at Violet's heart.

Sniffing and wiping tears from her face, Misty began to fight for control. Her voice wavered when she began speaking again. "We were on the pier at Rosarito Beach when they attacked us. They beat him. Those awful, wretched men beat him and then they held him and made him watch as they..." Misty closed her eyes, rocking back and forth on the bench. "After they were done with me they began beating him again. I begged them to stop. And they did. But only so they could tie his hands and feet..."

Misty had been facing the ocean, the conversation too painful to look Violet in the eye. But she turned her head and her sorrowful eyes gazed into Violet's compassion filled eyes. "They tied him up and threw him off the pier... into the ocean." The last three words seemed to take the very life out of her.

"Oh, Misty!" Violet pulled the girl into a fierce hug. The horrors this girl had lived through were almost too much for Violet's mind to grasp.

Misty returned the embrace with the same fierceness, and she clung to Violet as she continued telling her story. "He died. The only person who ever loved me… died. For a long time I didn't care about what happened to me. I had nothing to live for and I hoped one day the men would just decide to kill me, too."

Misty pulled away from Violet and stopped crying. She now sat tall, with her chin held high, dripping with tears. Filled with renewed strength she said, "But I am a mother now. I have so much to live for. And that's why you have to help me escape. Please say you will?"

"I, ah… I don't know what to do," Violet stammered.

"I begged my pimp to let me bleach my hair. Do you know why?"

The question filled Violet with a feeling of dread. "So you would look more like me?"

"Yes. This has to work. I don't think I believe in God, but if there is one, then this will have to work."

A chill settled over Violet. As she fought to keep the wind from blowing her hair into her face, she couldn't tell if it was the wind, or fear, that caused her to shiver. "How could I not help?" The words came out in a timid whisper.

Chapter 15

April 1994

Violet woke to the sound of her alarm clock. The abrasive noise jarred her from her fitful sleep. The night had been long, filled with strange dreams. Bits and pieces of her past had been seamed together in her restless mind to make a surreal reality in which her secret had been revealed.

Struggling to pull herself out of the dreams, she threw back the covers and silenced her alarm clock. With a yawn, she stood to dress.

Maybe she had made a huge mistake coming back to Mexico. Maybe Shawn was right. What would happen if her secret really was uncovered? She loved Nana Rosa and was coming to care for Everest as well. Her very presence could be placing them in danger if the wrong people found out about her past.

But wrong or right, the decision had been made and she was already here. The only option she had now was to press on. If she was careful, things would be ok. They had to be.

After pulling on a pair of jeans and a lightweight shirt, she simply needed to brush her hair and then she would be ready for the day. Spending a minimal amount of time on her thick, blonde hair, she pulled it into a high ponytail before leaving her room to join Nana Rosa in the kitchen to make breakfast.

Upon her arrival in the kitchen, Violet was surprised to see Mariela seated at the table. A wave of nausea rolled through her stomach. The young woman broke into a smile when she saw her and Mariela immediately began speaking to Violet. The young woman spoke in Spanish and Everest translated.

"She said she was hoping to see you. When Paul needed someone to bring us the grocery money for this month, she had volunteered. She wants to know what happened to you when you were kidnapped and if you know where her sister is. She hasn't been allowed to see her in a long time and she is worried."

Violet had a sinking feeling. If Mariela wanted to talk to her with Everest as a translator, keeping him from knowing too much would be impossible. As much as she longed to ask Mariela what she knew, Violet would simply have to end the conversation. It wasn't worth the risk of Everest getting involved.

"Tell her I am pleased to see her... " She hesitated, uncertain if she truly was pleased to see the young woman.

"But... please tell her that I don't know her sister. She must be mistaken."

Violet watched as he relayed the information. Mariela shook her head, it was apparent that she disagreed. Turning away from Everest, she looked at Violet and spoke again. As he interpreted, suspicion colored Everest's eyes.

"She insists she knows you. She said she would see you with her sister all the time." With his brow furrowed, he looked back and forth between the women. "Something doesn't add up here, Violet. What's going on?"

"Nothing, Everest!" Fighting to keep her voice calm, Violet tried to gain control of the conversation. "Honestly, I do not know her sister... and I don't know Mariela, either!"

Violet looked at Mariela and slowly said, "I'm sorry that you are worried about your sister, but I don't know who she is. I hope and pray that she is safe."

Mariela was confused and looked to Everest for him to interpret. But just like the last time, her reaction showed that she wasn't going to take that as an answer. And neither was Everest. He turned to her with gentle rebuke in his eyes.

"Look, Violet, I know you disobeyed Paul the last time you were here. He shared very little with me because he doesn't like to talk about the problems of other people, but I know enough about the situation to feel there is more to Mariela's claims than you are telling me."

Feeling like she was trapped, Violet looked at the door. She had to leave. "Yes, it's true that I made some mistakes the last time I was here. But that is none of your business. I promise to conduct myself better this time. Now, please,

I beg you to tell Mariela one last time that I regretfully cannot give her any information about her sister because I do not know who she is."

Reaching out a hand, she touched Mariela's shoulder and said, "I'm sorry...ah, lo siento."

Mariela just looked at her with sad eyes. Violet desperately wished she could just sit down and talk feely with her. But it was pointless. With the need for a translator, the only result would be bringing more people into a dangerous situation.

Violet turned back to Everest and held out her hand. "Please give me some of the money Mariela brought. I need to buy some groceries for lunch."

His sigh of resignation alerted Violet to the fact that he was just as frustrated as she was. But thankfully Everest wasn't the type to press someone for details so he let it go and handed her some money.

She felt great relief when she walked out the door, money in her pocket and a hastily written shopping list in her hand. With each step that took her from the soup kitchen, the less stressed she felt. With any luck, Mariela would give up and stop seeking information that Violet refused to give.

She was about half a block away from the supermarket when someone caught her eye. Intense emotions caused her whole body to tremble and she swallowed back nausea. It was him. Shawn was right. She hated to admit it, but he was right. She would recognize that man anywhere. Frank Smith was unforgettable, in a terrifying way.

Across the street, Frank Smith was leaning up against the wall of a pawn shop. He held a cigarette in one hand and a can of beer in the other. The mere sight of him was enough to bother her. But the fact that he was staring right at her with a menacing grin on his face shot fear through her heart. Memories of Rachel and all the terrible things Frank had done flashed through Violet's mind in rapid succession.

Violet wasn't even aware that she was still walking until she started to trip. She took her eyes off of Frank long enough to regain her balance. As soon as she stood tall again, she stopped walking so she could look at him again. She knew she should be running away, but she was compelled to look at him by the same strange force that would cause her to look at a train wreck.

But he was gone. The smoking cigarette butt that lay on the ground was the only evidence that he had indeed been there. *Was it really him? Or did I simply see someone who looked like him?*

Chapter 16

Violet was still trembling when she walked through the door of Mesa Vecindad. Uncertain as to whether she had actually seen Frank or not, she had rushed through her shopping, looking around her the whole time, wondering if he was following her. But when she stepped through the door and entered the soup kitchen, she was enveloped by the peace that seemed to permeate the place. And since she hadn't seen him more than that one time, she decided she had probably just been shaken up by seeing Mariela again. Her mind was probably playing tricks on her, bringing up more memories from her past than just the disturbing ones connected to Mexico. It probably wasn't him after all.

Sighing, Violet pushed the front door and it closed with a resounding thud that alerted the others of her return.

"Violet, is that you?" Everest asked from the kitchen.

"Yeah, I'm back."

Wondering if Everest needed something, Violet quickly walked into the kitchen. The first thing she saw was the apron he wore. "Wow, I didn't know aprons were proper attire for a Sasquatch." The playful remark seemed to conflict with the seriousness of the day. But it was a welcome break from her turbulent thoughts, and it filled her with a desire to simply forget her troubles. Thinking about the first time she had called him Sasquatch, she giggled a little. His initial response had been humorous, but each time she used her new nickname for him, he figured out a way to make her laugh even more.

This time, Everest raised his arms, bared his teeth and made an animal-like sound, pretending to be the Sasquatch she claimed he was. They both laughed at his antics and looks of fondness were exchanged between them.

"So I take it Mariela went back to The Mission?" Violet tentatively asked. She hadn't wanted to bring it up, but she also wanted to be reassured that the young woman wasn't going to be asking her any more questions today.

"You can be happy, she left right after you did... in tears."

A pang of guilt and compassion shot through her heart. With nothing to say in response, Violet simply looked at him and sighed. He pursed his lips and shrugged his shoulders as if he understood that Violet wasn't going to give in.

"On a different note... " Everest then turned and moved a stack of linens from the table. Behind them was another beautiful red rose. He grinned when he saw the surprise on her face. "Someone must be quite taken with you."'

And with those words, he simply left the room, just like last time.

Violet quickly walked to the table. Curiosity made her clumsy as she fumbled to open the card that came with the rose. Finally succeeding in opening it, she saw that it was written with the same neat penmanship.

"Unadorned beauty like yours is rare. I know why you are in Mexico. And you know why I can't think of anyone but you. S"

The message left her puzzled. Who was sending her these roses? And what did the S stand for? Could it be Shawn? Although she hadn't had any communication with him since she left the States, Violet admitted that it was possible he was the one sending her the roses. Maybe he was trying to make amends.

But the S could also be for Sasquatch. Everest had seemed to enjoy the fact that she used a nickname for him. Plus, he was there both times she had received the flowers. And both times he had walked away with a smile on his face as she reached to open the note.

Violet put the card back in the envelope and allowed her mind to mull over the facts. There had to be a way to figure out who the sender was. For a moment she thought maybe Frank should be added to the list of possible senders, after all, S could stand for Smith and she might have seen him watching her today. But she quickly dismissed that idea. Frank was so infatuated with Rachel, he probably would never move on.

Violet moved to the sink and began putting away the dishes that had been washed and set out to dry. She felt a little guilty for running out on Everest and Nana Rosa before she had prepared breakfast. Not only had she left them to make their own food, they had picked up the slack and washed the dishes even though it was her turn to wash today.

Remembering that she had skipped breakfast, she hurried to finish the dishes so she could find something to snack on. Her grumbling stomach wouldn't wait until lunch.

As she placed the last dish in the cupboard, she suddenly had a thought, "No!" The word came out in a shout without her even knowing it was going to happen. Santiago.

"It can't be him," she whispered, even though her mind told her otherwise.

Suddenly feeling weak, she made her way to the table and sat down. Violet searched her memory and decided that it most likely was him who was sending the roses. He knew why she was here; he understood her drive to help others. And even if he had meant it for other reasons, he was the one who told her to stay on at The Mission full-time.

But not only that, he also knew why she had left Mexico last time.

Why would he still think about me? Is it possible that he actually loved me? Does he even know what love is?

Chapter 17

December 1992

The day had been long and tiring. It was a day that felt like anything that could go wrong, did go wrong.

First, Anna had woken up feeling sick. And so Paul, insisting that she rest, had asked Violet to fill in for her and help the children with their studies. She had felt inadequate, but Paul had assured her that she would do just fine.

With a hurried rush to get everything ready for her day as substitute teacher, Violet was informed that she would need to take some new school supplies up to the school room with her when she went. She was almost to the top of the second floor stairs when the bottom of the box gave out. In a moment filled with the flutter of paper and the gentle thudding of crayons falling down the stairs, the box became completely empty as all of its contents were scattered everywhere. Feeling dismayed, Violet set the useless box down and shook her head. After running up to the school room to get some tape, she repaired the box, pushed up her sleeves and began picking things up.

By the time the mess was cleaned up and the papers put in proper order, everyone was behind schedule in their studies. So in order to make up for it, they had to work through a recess. The children were gracious and didn't complain too much, but since they worked through recess, Violet didn't have time to grade any of their work.

The rest of the day matched its frustrating start. The domino effect continued, one bad thing resulting in another bad thing. The minutes of the day seemed to drag out as one by one the children grew restless and fitful, tired of being patient with her since she wasn't completely sure what she was doing.

When the school day was finally over, Violet breathed a sigh of relief as the children ran outside to play. The playground was soggy from the winter rain earlier in the day, but at least the skies had cleared in time for the children to play a bit before dinner.

Violet breathed a breath of relief as she went down to the kitchen to help the cook prepare dinner. *Just a few more hours and I can be done with today.*

Thankfully, dinner was uneventful. But soon after everyone had eaten their fill and carried their plates to the kitchen sink, Bella started crying uncontrollably. There didn't appear to be anything wrong with the pudgy three year old, but try as he may, Paul was unable to console her.

Even though she was weary from the day, Violet offered to see if she could help. Scooping the child into her arms, Violet soothed her by patting Bella's back while rocking back and forth from one foot to the other.

Violet snuggled the girl close and began to sing. "How deep the Father's love for us, How vast beyond all measure..."

Verse after verse, Violet sang the words in her less than perfect voice. Her fatigue mixed with the emotions of holding a crying child and the truth of the words in her favorite hymn, causing her voice to break here and there.

A single tear rolled down Violet's cheek, leaving a wet trail. As if sensing Violet's tumbling emotions, Bella stopped her crying and pulled back from Violet. She reached out her little hand and wiped at the wetness on Violet's face.

"You no cry." The command was serious and Violet couldn't tell if the girl wanted her to be happy or if she was afraid she was going to have competition for sympathy. But when Bella spoke again, all doubt vanished and more tears sprung from Violet's eyes.

"No cry. Be happy, I love you." The girl smiled big, her wet eyelashes were dark and stuck together.

Violet couldn't help but smile in return. "Why were you crying, Bella?"

Bella's eye filled with tears again. "I miss my momma!"

Moved with compassion, Violet drew Bella back into her embrace. When Bella was just a little over two years old, her mother had dropped Bella off at The Mission and had never come back. Anna had told Violet how the mother was weeping, and it appeared she loved the child. But no one knew why Bella's mother felt it was necessary to leave her here. Sometimes parents simply couldn't afford another mouth to feed, and other times it was because the parents were seeking a new life in the States and couldn't take the children with them. It was a sad reality, but many of the children at The Mission actually had parents. Few were true orphans.

With her heart breaking for the child, Violet held Bella tightly and whispered into her hair, "It's okay. I love you. But even more, God loves you. It's okay, baby... It's okay."

The sun was set and the other children were already preparing for bed by the time Violet and Bella had stopped their tears. Bella had sobbed because she wanted a mother, Violet sobbed because she wished she could be that mother. Violet felt frustrated by the helpless feeling that over-powered the emotions bent on motherhood. She had nothing to offer Bella right now. As long as Bella still had a mother, all Violet could do was fill in for the woman until she returned. And who knew when, or if she ever would.

Was God calling her to stay here to fill that role of mother for Bella? The thought seemed too big to process right now. She was exhausted. She would have to think about it later, her focus needed to be on the task at hand. She needed to get Bella in bed, and then get some sleep herself.

As Violet pulled the covers up under her chin half an hour later, she was grateful the day was over, but she was even more grateful she had the day off tomorrow. Just minutes before she had sought the comfort of her own room,

Paul had come to Violet to tell her that Anna was feeling much better and they both felt she deserved some free time.

At first, she had protested, expressing her opinion that Anna should rest another day. But the day had left her so tired, with little to offer anyone. So she decided to stop protesting and simply express her thanks for their thoughtfulness.

With thoughts of spending long hours at the beach reading a book, Violet drifted off to sleep.

Chapter 18

Cool sand shifted beneath Violet's feet. The day wasn't as warm as Violet had hoped it would be, but it was still a beautiful day and she was soaking up every minute of her day off.

The night had been long. Though Bella had been soothed and calm when she went to bed, the poor little girl had woken several times throughout the night. The fact that Bella was missing her mom so much left Violet feeling upset on many levels.

Hoping to take a break from the things that were troubling her, Violet had brought a stack of books and a generous amount of stationery to her favorite place on the beach. It seemed like a good day to write to her friends and family.

The gentle scratching of pen on paper blended with the sound of the waves crashing. Despite all the evil things that went on just blocks away deeper in the city; there was real beauty and peace at Playa Del Sol.

This particular beach wasn't normally as busy as some of the other beaches that Violet had visited since her arrival in Tijuana. It had some shops around it, like the jewelry store that Violet enjoyed shopping at, but it seemed to be less touristy and more like a place the locals would go.

Looking across the beach to the old, beat up bench not too far away, Violet was reminded that this was the very spot Misty had asked her to meet her at.

The thought of Misty caused Violet's heart to drop. There had to be a way to help that girl without getting herself too involved. It was dangerous. But what was she supposed to do? Someone had to help, and if not Violet, then who?

Suddenly a gust of wind picked up the pages of the letter she was writing and sent them scattering across the sand. Throwing down the pen she was using, and pushing aside her thoughts of Misty, Violet stood up and rushed to gather the scattered pages. As she reached for them, the wind took them farther, causing her to run a few steps before trying again. Her fingers had brushed the edges of the paper several different times, but each time, they would start to move again and she almost gave up. A mix of frustration and humor washed over her as she imagined how silly she must look chasing after the fluttering papers.

By the time Violet had finally retrieved the scattered letter and returned to the spot where she had been sitting, she was pleasantly surprised to see Santiago stretched out in the sand next to her belongings.

"Santiago! How did you know I was here?"

His lazy smile made her tingle all the way from the tips of her toes up to the crown of her head. *Goodness he's handsome!*

"'How did I know?' she asks. Where else would you be?" He laughed good-naturedly and the sound of it reminded Violet of a babbling brook. In that moment, joy seemed to pour so naturally from his smiling mouth. Watching him tease her reminded her of how much fun he was. The only time she had ever seen him in a solemn mood was that day at the beach when he had asked her what drove her out of bed each morning. She didn't know why that conversation was different than any of the others they'd had, but there was a definite difference to his demeanor then. *Something, maybe a burden of guilt, dwells deep within him, and whatever it is has caused him great sorrow.*

Looking at the happy man sitting before her, Violet decided that even though serious and solemn moments were a part of life, she liked the teasing, smiling Santiago better. After all, wasn't any person more fun to be around when they were smiling? Maybe given enough time, he would open up to her and share his burden, allowing her to help him overcome it.

As she sat down next to him, he shifted his weight to lessen the space between them. "When I stopped by The Mission looking for you, Paul said you had taken the day off. He said you had walked to the beach. And since I know which one is your favorite, well, it was pretty easy to find you."

"How come you're not working today? Do you have the day off too?"

"Actually, I came here because I wanted to tell you something." Santiago reached out and took Violet's hand. He rubbed his thumb back and forth on the top of her small white fingers. "Violeta, I am falling in love with you."

The declaration surprised her. Had he said anything else — anything at all — she couldn't have been more surprised. How long had they known each other? Certainly not long enough to be in love. He felt feelings of deep affection maybe, but not love. Pulling her hand out of his, she stared at him, searching for a fitting reply. But nothing came to her mind. And so she said the only thing she could think to say. "What?"

"I said I am falling in love with you." Santiago was completely calm; in fact, he seemed to be taking great joy in the reaction his words had caused.

"You can't be serious! We barely know each other. In fact, I don't even know what your last name is! And you don't know anything about my family… or how old I am… or… or if I snore!"

Laughing that same bubbling laugh as before, Santiago reached out and tried to capture her hand again. "Slow down! I didn't propose or anything. I simply said I am falling in love with you."

Violet slapped at his hand, refusing to let him touch her.

"Seriously Violeta, I don't care if you snore. You could snore so loud a person would think a freight train was passing through the room, it doesn't matter."

While he spoke, Violet eyed him with a smirk on her face. And when he stopped talking, she just looked at him, waiting for him to continue.

"Look, all I know is you are beautiful. Unadorned, unaltered, you are stunningly beautiful. You love God. You are kind." As he spoke, Santiago took hold of her hand. His flattering words of admiration had caused her to drop her defenses and she forgot to resist his touch.

"You are like music pouring from a skilled pianist's hands; you thrill anyone near you." While he was still holding her hand in his, Santiago scooted over until he was close enough to put his other arm around her.

He was so close she could smell a slight fragrance of soap and aftershave. He smelled good and she wanted to lean in closer and freely enjoy the moment. But something inside her was starting to panic. So what if he smelled good and told her she was pretty? Things were moving too fast and she needed to know more about him before she could let either of them fall in love.

Violet shook her head as if to wake herself up. She put her hand on his chest to push him away. It had seemed like a good idea, but he was strong and unmoving. Instead of breaking free from the spell she felt like she was under, she now had her hand on his chest and could feel his muscles through the thin fabric of his cotton shirt. Her fingertips felt as if they had a mind of their own as they began to play with the buttons on his shirt.

Closing her eyes, Violet sighed. Summoning all her will power, she pushed away from him with more force than before. She rose to her feet as he pulled back.

"I know practically nothing about you! I need to know more. What's your last name?"

Santiago remained sitting and looked up at her. "Look, I want to tell you everything about me. And I will. But I can't right now."

"Do you know how ridiculous that sounds? Why can't you tell me something as simple as your last name? This is stupid!" Violet was angry now. With hurried, rough movements, she began to pick up her books and letters, shoving them into her handbag.

Santiago rose to his feet and once again reached for her hand. "Listen, I promise you that I will tell you anything you want to know. Later… when I can." Squeezing her hand, he looked into her eyes. They were sincere, filled with emotion. "If I tell you right now, then things with my work could be compromised. I have plans that include you but the timing has to be right. I just need you to trust me."

Pulling her hand up to his lips, he kissed it as he asked "Can you just trust me?"

"I… no. Santiago, you are asking…"

Before Violet could finish her sentence, he pulled her body tightly to his and passionately kissed her lips. Torn between returning the kiss and slapping him across the face for his boldness, Violet wrestled herself from his embrace. Turning her back to him, she picked up her bag and then started to walk away.

"Violeta, you know I am a Christian man. You know I love God and want to serve Him, we talked about that the last time we saw each other. Please..." He took a few steps, going after her. "Just stop. Please, let's talk this through."

Violet stopped walking and turned back around. "I can't be near you until you are willing to open up." The words poured from her lips with practical truth.

She was shaking. Never in her life had she imagined this would happen. She was supposed to feel elated and blissful when a handsome man told her he loved her. But dreams were different than reality and right now she felt anything but blissful or elated. She felt sickeningly torn between her physical response to him and her practical defense against lustful sin.

"Until you can talk freely with me, you have no right to be kissing me, let alone making declarations of... of... love." Her voice broke as she forced out the last word. Fresh anger boiled up inside while sadness swept over her as she took a deliberate step away from him.

He tried to defend himself, but she refused to listen. Tears blurred her eyes, making it hard to see. She closed her eyes to stop the tears and reached up her hands to wipe away the ones that had already fallen. She continued to walk while she did this, afraid that if she stopped walking she would change her mind and run back into his arms.

For a brief moment, she walked as if completely blind while her hands furiously worked at removing the tears from her eyelashes. When she brought her hands down, she saw Misty running toward her.

"Violet! What happened? Why are you crying?" Concern was displayed in her pretty face.

Violet ignored the girl's questions and asked her own instead, "What are you doing here?"

"I came looking for you. We need to talk, make plans. I don't have... " Misty's voice trailed off as her eyes grew large. Her focus was on something behind Violet and whatever it was must have been pretty awful because the girl began to tremble in fear.

Violet turned to look behind her. But the action left her puzzled because the only thing she saw was Santiago walking toward them; there was nothing to be afraid of. As Violet turned back to Misty to ask her what was wrong, the girl grabbed her by the arm and pulled her. The force of Misty's pulling caused Violet to lurch forward, her bag slipping from her shoulder and resting heavily on her forearm, but she didn't fix it.

"We have to go right now!" Misty insisted. "Come on, Violet!"

The girl's urgency confused Violet and she stubbornly pulled against Misty refusing to move. "What is it? What's going on?"

"That man behind you... " Misty yanked Violet's arm, causing her to drop her bag as she was forced to take a step to keep from falling. "That man! He works with my pimp."

Chapter 19

Violet couldn't breathe. Rage blazed a red hot trail through her heart, leaving her chest tight and constricted. But her fear blazed just as hot, paralyzing her with its panic-inducing heat.

Sinking to the ground, Violet struggled to get her emotions under control. She couldn't tell what bothered her the most, the fact that Santiago had been lying to her, or the fact that she had believed him. Shouldn't she have seen through his lies?

Gasping for air, she tried to take a breath. She needed to breathe.

Silent sobs wracked her body. *I'm a failure. I tried so hard, but I am no different than Vivian. But is it really a surprise?* She had always been fascinated by men and a part of her longed for the thrill of being around people who casually viewed sex.

It was just a matter of time… I was bound to be caught up with an evil man.

Her disappointment in herself grew until it crowded out all other thoughts as she continued her struggle to breathe. She was unaware of Misty's pleading for her to stand up and run away. And she didn't even notice how Santiago gently moved Misty away so he could pull her into his arms.

"Violeta! Breathe! Come on, you have to calm down and take a breath!" Santiago spoke sternly as he carefully shook her, scared by the blue that was tinging her lips. He turned to Misty and demanded an explanation. "What happened? What did you say to her?"

Misty simply looked at him. Her large brown eyes filled with tears and fear.

Santiago looked back to the woman in his arms, and gently shook her again, shouting at her to breathe. His actions pulled her from her shock. Finally taking a full breath, Violet looked around as if seeing Misty and Santiago for the first time.

Suddenly, Violet started hitting Santiago. "Liar! You're a pimp!" she screamed as she hit him over and over. "Get away from me! I never want to see you again!"

"Violeta, I... " Santiago looked confused.

Filled with rage and the sting of betrayal, Violet slapped him across the face to stop him from defending himself. The blow stunned him and he rocked back on his heels, one hand on his cheek, the other trying to steady himself.

Springing up, Violet grabbed up her bag, took Misty's hand and began running.

"Stop, Violeta! I need you!" Santiago yelled as he got up from the ground and started after the girls. "I had plans for you to be …"

Violet stopped running. Turning to look at him, she held out her hand, stopping him mid-sentence. "I'm sure you had lots of plans for me! Don't you dare come near me again."

"But… "

"I mean it!" she yelled, angrier than she had ever been in her life. "I let you tempt me into kissing you! I almost believed you when you said you cared about me."

The pain of a broken heart and broken dreams welled in her eyes, and spilled out to make wet trails down her face. With a voice that warbled and cracked, she said, "What a fool I am."

Santiago ran a hand through his dark hair, frustration evident in his every move. "I do care, dang it!"

"I'm sure you do… but not for me. You only care about my 'unadorned beauty 'and how that works into your plans. What were you going to do, paint me up to make me look even better… is that what all this was really about? Sex and money?"

Santiago's eyebrows came together in confusion and he shook his head. "What are you talking about? Sex and money… what?"

"Forget it! Don't waste your time trying to act innocent." She looked at him with contempt. "Now, let us leave and don't follow. I never want to see you again."

When Violet and Misty turned around and started to walk away, she heard Santiago yell in frustration.

It sounded as if his heart were ripping in two. But Violet closed her ears and refused to be moved by his pain; she was certain his sorrow was from losing a new "item" to sell rather than a broken heart. No, men like him didn't have the ability to love.

Thankful that Misty had come when she did, Violet trembled just thinking what would have happened had she allowed Santiago to sweet talk her into believing he really did love her. She had come frighteningly close to being in the same circumstances as Misty and the other girls. The thought caused bile to rise in her throat. To be used by men night after night, but never once knowing what it was to be truly loved was surely the worst kind of pain a woman could feel.

Squeezing Misty's hand as they ran, Violet was acutely aware of two very important things she needed to do. First, she needed to remove Santiago from her life. Second, she had to do whatever it took to get Misty away from her pimp.

The girls' footsteps fell hard and loud on the aged and crumbling blacktop of the street. As she let Misty lead her away from Santiago and the beach, Violet's practical mind began processing the two thoughts. She had to find a way to make amends for her stupidity concerning Santiago. And she had to start making plans to help Misty be fully redeemed from the lifestyle that had been forced upon her.

Chapter 20

April 1994

Violet woke to the deep, throaty sound of a man screaming and the jarring sound of dishes shattering. With her heart pounding in her chest, she pushed herself up in the bed, throwing the blanket off. *It's happened. They found out and have come to get me. Shawn was right! It was stupid to even come here!*

With adrenaline pumping, she hurriedly put her slippers on, shrugged into a sweatshirt and started to run toward the sound. But she suddenly stopped and walked back into her bedroom.

Looking around the small room, she searched for something she could use as a weapon. Feeling the need to hurry, she scanned and scanned, but couldn't find anything that would be suitable to fend off a man who was bent on harming the people in this house.

I need a weapon! What can I use? God, show me what I should do... Please don't let anything happen to Everest or Nana Rose because of me!

As the silent prayer passed through her mind, Violet's eyes came to rest on the small table beside her bed. It was old and rickety, if she applied enough pressure to one of the legs, it was sure to come off. It wouldn't be as effective as a gun or a knife, but it would certainly work well to club someone in the head. All she would have to do is break it off the table and then sneak up on whoever was attacking Everest. If she hit the man hard enough, she might be able to knock him out. It was worth a try.

Hearing more screams and crashes from the kitchen, Violet jumped to action.

Running to the table, she quickly swept her arm across the top of it. Books went flying with their pages fluttering. A plastic cup landed on the floor, spilling its contents and leaving a puddle next to the books. Violet quickly checked each leg, trying to find one that was loose. When they all seemed to be the same, she chose one and yanked as hard as she could. It gave a little, but remained attached. Turning the table on its side, she placed one foot on the leg while balancing herself with a hand on the wall. With swift, yet careful movements, she picked her foot up off the floor to stand on the leg. After a loud crack, the leg broke free and Violet slumped against the wall.

After taking a moment to steady her shaking hands and catch her breath, she bent down, grasped the piece of wood and ran for the door.

Nearing the kitchen, she readied herself for a fight.

But when she looked through the door and into the kitchen, she sagged in relief. Instead of seeing a catastrophic fight between good and evil, she simply saw Everest holding up a mouse trap. Pots and pans were strewn about with shards of broken dishes scattered on the floor. A dead mouse hung limp from the trap in Everest's hand, ensnared by the peanut butter that had been used for bait.

Violet leaned against the doorframe as her rush of adrenaline abated, leaving her weak and shaking. Feeling a bit silly for over-reacting, she breathed a prayer of thanks.

Everest was doing a strange mix of dancing and jumping while shaking his whole body in a dramatic display of disgust.

"Yuck! Gross!"

Holding the edge of the trap, he tried to walk outside. But after only two steps, he started to scream again. "It just moved! Ah! It's going to touch me!"

Violet began to laugh as she saw him gag. Her laughter caught his attention and he stared at her in embarrassment.

Rushing to his side with her makeshift club still clutched in her hand, she reached out and took the trap from him with her free hand. "Seriously? Sasquatch is bothered by dead mice?"

Everest pursed his lips and ducked his head. Violet couldn't tell if he was genuinely that embarrassed, or just teasing her.

"Just take it away!" he demanded, too upset to respond to the nickname. "And for your information, I saw another one. And it was quite alive."

"But what should I do with it? Throw it in the trash, or bury it?"

Everest shuddered again. "Oh, disgusting! Don't throw it in the trash, it will stink! Just toss it outside and I'll bury it later."

Violet walked toward the back door of the house. Looking over her shoulder she said, "Are you sure? It looks as if you might lose your lunch if you try to bury this thing!"

Everest gave her a scathing glare before joining in her mirth. "Well, it's a good thing it's morning. Lucky for me... I haven't eaten lunch yet."

Violet rolled her eyes and shook her head. Walking out the door, she quickly placed the mouse-filled trap by the trash can. Giddiness rose up in her and she started to giggle. The morning's events had shaken her up, but now that she knew there was no danger, the relief that poured over her caused her to feel like a silly elementary school girl trying not to laugh during class. Poor Everest was really scared of mice!

But the more she tried to stop laughing, the worse it got until finally she just stopped trying to control it and laughed out loud for several minutes.

Making an effort to choke back her laughter, she walked back into the kitchen with just the hint of a smile on her face. Even though she found his actions funny, she didn't want to hurt his feelings. And she figured she had already laughed at him enough.

"I heard you laughing out there. Just wait... next time it will be you who finds a fat and ugly mouse murdered right where you keep your favorite coffee cup!"

Everest's feigned indignation dissolved Violet's ability to refrain from laughing. First, her shoulders began to shake as she tried desperately to hold it back. Then, her lips started to curl. And finally, a howling laugh escaped her mouth as she reached out to touch Everest's arm.

"Oh Sas... I'm sorry." She squeaked out the words between giggles. "But you should have seen yourself!"

With just a small smile, Everest shook his head. It was obvious that he too, was amused, but he tried to look annoyed. "Great, now I have an even worse nickname... since when does Sasquatch evolve to just Sas?"

"When... " Violet laughed, wiping tears from her eyes.

"When the person who made the nickname becomes lazy!"

Suddenly, Everest's expression turned serious. Looking at Violet with curiosity, he said "What's that in your hand?"

Looking down at the table leg, she marveled that her fingers were still wrapped around its smooth finish. *How could I have forgotten I am holding that?*

"Oh... well, when I woke to your over-dramatic screaming, I thought you were being attacked. So my nightstand made the ultimate sacrifice to be the weapon that saved your life." All her feelings of mirth had disappeared and she struggled to sound lighthearted.

As Violet's explanation rushed out of her nervous mouth, Everest stood taller; his whole body became alert as questions filled his eyes. "Why would you think I was being attacked?"

Shifting from one foot to the other, Violet nervously tried to think of a way to direct the conversation away from where Everest was sure to take it. "Well, who would have thought someone would scream so much over a mouse?"

"You're stalling. What is it, Violet? People don't just assume they should grab a weapon before running to see why a person in the next room screams. Does this have something to do with the secret you're keeping? Are you... "

Everest blinked rapidly as if he were trying to keep up with the thoughts accumulating in his brain. "Are we... in danger?"

Looking him in the eye, she saw nothing but concern in his eyes. There was no judgment, no condescension, just genuine caring.

Maybe it's time. Maybe I should just tell him.

Standing there, swinging the table leg back and forth, Violet fought with herself. All the reasons for her secrecy swarmed in her mind like bees when their hive is disturbed.

"I think everyone was right." Speaking those words cost her greatly. It was as if she were admitting defeat. For over a year she had strived to overcome what had happened; she'd promised herself that she could still be a missionary to the people she loved here in Tijuana. But, just like her efforts to protect herself from the lustful, foolish desires of her heart, she had failed yet again. It was time to admit it, and simply move on. "I'll begin the arrangements; I'll leave at sunrise tomorrow."

Everest was clearly stunned. He stammered for a few seconds and finally spit out a word. "No!"

The emotions that filled his eyes scared Violet. She hadn't been prepared to see so much caring, so much fondness there. She couldn't allow him to express those feelings; it was too much to deal with.

Like all the other times in her life when things got hard, she chose to just walk away.

Everest was still trying to persuade her to stay, but she closed her ears and refused to hear him. To anyone watching, she would have appeared coldhearted and unfeeling. But that couldn't have been farther from the truth. She was dying inside.

Chapter 21

Tears streamed down Violet's face and she made no effort to wipe them away. She had told Everest she was going to make arrangements for her flight home, but instead, she found herself walking the beach.

Though she knew she couldn't stay any longer, she couldn't bring herself to make the decision final. Every fiber of her being longed to stay and minister here. Mesa Vecindad and The Mission were places where people's lives were being changed — where she was being changed. And she liked the changes God was making.

A seagull flew over her. The gentle breeze played with her hair. All around her there were things that spoke of peace and calm.

The repetitive roar of the waves lapping at the sand tried to numb her heart and ease the pain she was feeling. But she felt no peace, and she still longed for something to lessen the searing pain racing through her chest.

She loved being here and watching as her faith grew deeper and stronger each day. But if she stayed, she had to keep her secret. And the changes this place had worked in her heart caused her to hate the secret she had buried so deep. She longed to break the silence; she longed to be free from it all.

Just last night, before going to sleep, she had been reading her Bible. She was in the book of John, and when she got to the 32nd verse of Chapter 8, she had been touched. Jesus had said, "Then you will know the truth, and the truth will set you free."

That verse placed in her an intense desire for the freedom Jesus was talking about. She understood that He was talking to the Jews who believed in Him, and the truth that Jesus was talking about referred to himself. But she was struck with the thought that she was living in contradiction because in the verse before, Jesus had also said, "If you hold to my teaching, you are really my disciples."

How could she claim to be holding to Jesus' teachings when she was placing herself in situations where she would have to lie? It didn't matter if she stayed here and served at Mesa Vecindad or The Mission, if she was lying to those around her, then she wasn't obeying Jesus' teachings.

That knowledge had slammed into her heart with a life-changing force. Her desire to serve God and to be His disciple was compromised by her secret. And since she couldn't safely share what had happened when she was here the last time, she'd felt frustrated and at a loss.

She had gone to sleep last night asking God to show her what she should do about it.

And now this. Her knee-jerk reaction and assumption that Everest was in danger, attested to the fact that things were not right. Everest needed to know what had caused her panic this morning. As her ministry partner, he deserved to know.

As she walked the beach, she felt torn. It was a troubling situation. Secrecy had become something she hated. But what choice did she have? The secret didn't involve just her; if that had been the case, she would have broken her silence long before now. But it did involve others. And if her fear this morning was any reflection of reality, then just her presence here was placing everyone in danger.

With a heavy, burdened heart, Violet decided it was time to go back to Mesa Vecindad. Whether she wanted to or not, she had to start packing. It was time to go home.

· ∘ ◉◦ ∘ ·

When Violet walked through the front door of Mesa Vecindad, she was a little apprehensive. It was quite possible that Everest was going to see her and press her for answers.

Uncertain what she should do, she carefully closed the door and just stood there.

The upbeat tempo of a popular worship song could be heard coming from Everest's room. The static and constant low hum testified to the fact that he was listening to the radio; and judging by the artist who was singing, it most likely was a radio station from the States.

The music seemed to wrap around her, filling her with nostalgia. *Shawn loves this song.*

In her mind she could picture the last time she had seen him sing it. The tough and muscular policeman was transformed when he worshipped God. The sight of Shawn with his red head tilted up toward the sky, eyes closed and singing with abandon, had been one of the most endearing things she had ever seen.

With a pang in her heart, Violet admitted that she desperately loved him. She needed to make things right between them. She wanted to be his wife, she wanted to spend her years watching him worship God.

Letting out a sigh of determination, Violet acknowledged yet again, the truth that it was time to leave Tijuana. She had to ask Shawn to forgive her and most importantly, she had to confide in him her darkest fears and her deepest secret.

Just the thought of the work ahead of her left her exhausted and nervous. She had no way of knowing what his reaction would be, but she knew in the long run it would all be worth it. She should never have left home with things the way they were.

Cringing, Violet thought of all the people she had hurt as she had stubbornly demanded to have her own way.

She was still standing by the door when a knock startled her. Adrenaline rushed through her body much the same as it had this morning when she'd heard Everest's screams.

Placing a hand over her heart as if the action could calm its frantic beating, she opened the door.

Standing before her was the same florist who had been there before. She wore the same apron and in her hand she held what looked like the same red rose.

This time, instead of asking for Violet, the woman simply smiled and said, "For you."

"Gracias." Violet took the vase from the woman's hand and dipped her head in a greeting and farewell all rolled into one.

Almost expecting Everest to be watching from the hallway, Violet looked around the house as she walked into the kitchen and placed the vase on the table. She absentmindedly noticed that everything had been put back in place and the broken dishes had been swept up.

With a tremor of excitement, she took the pale yellow envelope from the vase and opened it. This time, in the same neat handwriting, the tiny card said,

"If I could just talk to you, if we could just be alone, you would see how wonderful things could be. S."

Something about the phrase caused Violet to remember the letters and cards that Frank used to send her friend. Was Frank really here? Was it possible that since Rachel had a protective stalking order placed against him that Frank had decided to start stalking her instead?

But just as quickly as the thought had been formed, it was dismissed. The only logical sender of the roses would be either Shawn or Santiago. Hadn't she walked away from both men as they begged to talk to her?

But just this morning as she'd walked away from him, Everest had begged to talk to her, too.

Still hearing the music coming from his room, Violet knew Everest was here. Taking confident steps down the hall, she rehearsed what she was going to say to him.

As her knuckles knocked on his door, her heart raced. If he was the one sending the roses, it was time for her to know.

Chapter 22

When Everest opened the door, he looked annoyed. And for a moment, Violet wondered if maybe she should have just left things alone.

Clearing her throat, she willed herself to stop feeling nervous. "Hey, uh... I wanted you to know that I'm back."

Instead of answering, Everest just looked at her. He blinked slowly, still obviously annoyed.

Clearing her throat again, Violet decided to try to make amends. "So, look... I'm sorry. I'm sorry I freaked out this morning and broke the table. I'll replace it before I go, I promise. But more than the table, I'm sorry that I can't tell you what's going on."

"An apology isn't what I was hoping for Violet," Everest sighed. "What I was hoping was that you would say you had changed your mind. I was hoping you would stay."

"I can't." Violet paused, trying to think of some way to bridge the gap that had formed between them this morning. "It's a long, long story. A story I can't tell you."

"Why?"

Violet looked him in the eye and shook her head just the tiniest bit. "I'm so tired of hearing people ask me that. I can't tell you because... because you are better off not knowing. If I tell you, then you're part of it and if someone comes around asking questions, then you will have to start lying as well."

She closed her eyes as fresh guilt washed over her and whispered. "Believe me, keeping secrets and lying aren't habits you want to start."

"Okay. Fair enough. But... " Everest took a tentative step toward her. His hand moved as if to reach out and grasp hers, but he stopped that from happening. "That's it then. You're leaving, just like that?"

Everest's demeanor had changed from annoyed to sad. "Can I say or do anything to make you change your mind?"

"I don't know about changing my mind, but there is something you can do for me."

"What's that?"

Gathering all the courage she could find, Violet decided it was now or never. "You can tell me if you are the one who's been sending those roses."

Everest looked stunned. His eyes were large and a smile flittered across his face. "No. No, I never even thought to do something like that. Does this mean you got another one?"

At first, Violet wasn't sure whether she was disappointed or relieved to learn that Everest wasn't responsible for the roses. But as she tried to understand what that information meant, she realized she felt a little of both. There was a distinct disappointment over the fact that she wasn't much closer to figuring out the mystery than she was before. But she was also very relieved. If Everest was indeed the one sending the roses, then she would have to find a way to gently explain to him that she was still very much in love with Shawn. And it would be hard to make him understand that truth because when they had gone out for tacos that night, she hadn't been very kind when she had talked about Shawn. She had still been allowing her anger to control her, and the result didn't paint Shawn in a very good light.

"Yes. I did get another, just a few minutes ago actually."

"So you don't know who's sending them? I thought you did. I had assumed Shawn was trying to make amends."

"Maybe he is," Violet agreed. But she couldn't help thinking it was probably Santiago instead.

As if hearing her thoughts, Everest said, "Who else would it be?"

A nervous laugh escaped her lips. "You're right. Who else could it be? Well, anyway, now that we have that out of the way, I'll go start packing."

"You really are going?" It was a statement more than a question. "Would it have changed anything if I was the one who had sent the roses?"

"No." The word came out on a weary whisper. "No, it wouldn't."

"Just call him." Everest sounded as weary as she felt.

Violet was confused. "Who?"

"Shawn. You still love him, don't you?" When Violet started to ask him how he knew, he waved his hand and said, "Your eyes lit up when I said his name just then. You're pretty easy to read when you're not trying to hide something."

"But I will be home soon; wouldn't it be better to tell him in person?"

"Violet, just call the man."

Knowing Everest was right, Violet nodded and simply walked away.

◦ ◦ ◉◉◉ ◦ ◦

After failing to reach Shawn at his home number, Violet decided to call the police station. A feeling of irritation fluttered through her mind as she realized she had been out of contact with Shawn long enough that he must have a new work schedule. Normally, at this time of night he would be home.

Waiting for dispatch to answer, Violet rehearsed what she was going to say to Shawn when she finally reached him. Would it be better to apologize right away or to tell him she loved him first?

"Caspar Police, how can I help you?" The perky woman's voice broke through Violet's thoughts.

"Can I speak with Officer Shawn Sinclair please?"

"Can I ask who's calling?"

"It's Violet Thompson."

"Oh, Violet! How are you? We've all missed you here at the station. But no one has missed you as much as Shawn!"

The woman's voice sounded familiar to Violet, but she had no idea who she was talking to. She was tempted to ask, but decided it didn't really matter. And since the woman seemed to assume that Violet knew her, it would be awkward to ask for her name. "I'm good. But I really need to talk to Shawn. Is he there?"

"Oh, sweetie, didn't he tell you?"

Impatience surged forth and Violet had to bite back a snide remark. "Tell me what?"

"He left town yesterday. Shawn has gone on vacation to Tijuana! Lucky man."

As Violet thanked the woman and hung up the phone, she smiled. *Shawn is coming to see me!*

Running to her room, Violet sprawled out on her bed. In her emotional turmoil today, she had forgotten that she didn't have a suitcase. So instead of packing tonight, she would have to wait until tomorrow when she could go buy something. But maybe that was for the best. With Shawn coming to Mesa Vecindad, who knew what tomorrow would bring.

Thoughts of Shawn traveling to Tijuana so he could declare his undying love for her filled Violet's mind and warmed her heart as she went to sleep that night. And for the first time in a long time, the dreams she dreamt were pleasant ones filled with happiness and joy.

Chapter 23

The day had just begun when Shawn bounded through the door of Mesa Vecindad. Everest had been the one to greet him and when Violet walked through the kitchen door, she was surprised at the tension between the two men. But it didn't take long to see that Shawn was angry. A fleeting thought of compassion for Everest passed through Violet's mind as she wondered what Shawn might have said to him.

Turning to her, Shawn said "Do you know how long it took me to find this place? You've been foolish, Violet. You should have told me where you were!"

In spite of the way his presence made her heart flutter and her mind feel like melted butter, her own anger flared at his words. "It's nice to see you, too!" She bit off the words, letting disrespectful sarcasm color them. "And, for your information, I am not a fool!"

Spinning around, Violet turned her back on Shawn and stormed into the kitchen.

"Oh, no you don't! I've had just about enough of you walking away from me." Shawn was close on her heels while Everest watched the display with a mixture of concern and amusement on his face.

"Well, I've had just about enough of your bullying! How dare you walk in here and call me a fool? If you had taken the time to get off your high horse and actually talk to me, you might have had time to hear me say I am sorry and that I still love you!"

Shawn's anger dissipated, leaving him awkward and meek. A slight pink tinged his cheeks and Violet thought he looked a bit embarrassed. "Do you mean it? Do you still love me?"

"Of course I do! You may be annoyingly bossy and always on 'cop mode', but I can't help it... " Violet leaned in toward Shawn, eager to bridge the gap between them. It had been so long since she had seen him last and she longed to be wrapped in those strong arms. "I love you more than I ever thought I could love someone. And until you came crashing in here, I was going to apologize for the way I handled things when I left home."

In a matter of seconds, Shawn was holding her. His lips were demanding as they found her mouth. But the tenderness that was so characteristic of Shawn was still there and despite the demanding nature of the kiss, Violet felt safe, secure and cherished.

When Shawn broke the kiss, he pulled back just enough to speak. "You scared the tar out of me! I went to The Mission and they said you weren't there. When they told me how to get here, I just about lost my composure. This place is so stinking hard to find, it looks just like a regular house! The neighborhood isn't as good as where The Mission is... And you're too close to that street, Vi. I could never live with myself if something had happened to you. That's why you have to listen to me; you can't stay here."

Violet was on full alert now, pushing away from him she said, "Wait, what street are you talking about?"

"Calle Escondido."

At the name, Violet's whole body went cold. How did he know the name of the street where her life became ensnared in danger? And even though she had planned to share her secret with him, the fact that he already knew something about it filled her with an inexplicable feeling of betrayal. Defensiveness rose up in her again. "You came all this way to tell me to go home?"

"Not exactly, but... yes. You need to go home. You shouldn't be here; you should never have come back."

"I can't believe you!"

"Look. I love you. I still want to marry you. That's why I care, that's why I'm here."

"How can you say that? I thought you wanted to be free from me and my problems." Her last comment was once again laced with disrespectful sarcasm. As the words flowed from her mouth, she knew they were unfair and hurtful, but she didn't care. "There's no way you can marry me if you don't trust me. And you know what? I was actually starting to think you were right. Did you know I was actually supposed to buy a ticket today and fly home? I was going to go home and ask for your forgiveness."

Violet took a hand and pushed back the strand of hair that had escaped her pony tail and fallen in her eyes. She stubbornly continued her defensive argument. "You think I'm foolish? You're the fool. You wasted your time coming here, I was going home anyway. If you would have simply called me, you would have known that!"

Shawn was speechless. Violet watched as he tried to make sense of what she had just said. After a moment, he cleared his throat and said, "I didn't come here to call you a fool. I'm sorry. That was not the best choice of words."

Violet stood her ground and just looked at him, waiting to hear what he was going to say next.

"I came here to tell you that I love you. That I want to work things out. But more than that, I came to warn you that Frank is here. It's been confirmed. He's been seen on Calle Escondido, that's why you're not safe being so close to that street."

"Oh!" Violet gasped. "But he's not here for me. He's just here because of what he did that night... I still can't believe..." A rush of emotions caused Violet's throat to tighten. What Frank had done to Jacob was heartbreaking, terrible, and cruel. She wished the police would find him and make him pay for his actions.

Shawn was holding her once again, soothing her as tears sprung to her eyes. "He may or may not be here because of you. But I'm begging you. You can't stay here."

"Okay."

Violet knew eventually she would have to tell Shawn the real reason why Calle Escondido was a dangerous place for her to be near. But for now, as she snuggled close to his chest, she was content to let Shawn think that Frank was their biggest problem. There would be plenty of time later on to finally tell him her secret.

"Good. Go get your things. I need to meet up with a friend of mine who has a lead on Frank and then I will get you on a plane."

"Wait." Surprise caused Violet to pull away from his comforting embrace. Looking him in the eye, she said, "You're not coming with me?"

"No. I have to stay here and see this through."

"I thought you were here on vacation. You can't spend your vacation working; come with me and we can just forget about everything for a while. I want to be with you."

Pulling her close again, he rested his cheek on the top of her head. Shawn sighed and said, "I want to be with you, too. But I took time off from work to be here. I need to track Frank down. There's this feeling in my gut that says we're in for some trouble if we don't find him. I couldn't get the Sarge to agree with me. So I am not officially here. I'm vacationing here and if I just happen to find something out, well, that would be all right with me!"

"How sneaky!" Violet giggled.

"No, I'm not trying to be sneaky, Violet. I'm just concerned and my hands are tied. For Rachel's sake, I owe it to her to see this thing through. And if that means I lose my job, so be it. There's no telling what Frank Smith is going to do next; he must be stopped."

A rustling sound caused both Violet and Shawn to turn and look. There, standing in the doorway of the kitchen was Everest.

"I hate to interrupt your argument, or making up, or whatever it is that you two are doing. But I couldn't help overhearing what you were saying, Shawn. If you need a place to stay while you're in Tijuana, you're more than welcome to stay here."

Violet looked from one man to the other and then quickly said, "That settles it! Shawn can stay here and with the protection of two men, I don't need to go home!" Looking up at Shawn with love-struck eyes, she said, "Then I can spend more time with you!"

"Violet. Stop." Shawn commanded. "You are indeed going home. And I'm not staying here."

Shawn turned to look at Everest. "It is a very kind offer and I am very appreciative, but I'm not here in Tijuana for light reasons. Like I said to Violet, Frank is a dangerous man. And I don't want Mesa Vecindad to be involved in this. Just the fact that I am here could be enough to bring about trouble for you."

Shawn's words rang with truth. Truth that left Violet filled with guilt. Why did she want to be here so much when the result could mean danger for those around her?

Chapter 24

It had been a busy morning. After the initial plans of how and when Violet was to go home were in place, Shawn and Violet had gone in search of a suitcase and a night stand to replace the one she had broken. Violet had told Shawn the whole story about turning the table leg into a weapon, thinking it was humorous, but Shawn failed to see the humor. Instead, he had replied with a very typical answer for a man in law enforcement. Then he gave her a long lecture about being prepared, owning a gun for protection, and how he was going to give her shooting lessons when they got home.

Violet understood where he was coming from, but none of those things were appealing to her. However, she was going to marry him, so she needed to appreciate the way he saw things and let him lead her. He had a strong desire to protect her and he would expect her to learn to protect herself as well. Both of which were very good things, even if they were boring.

After they had found a small nightstand and a suitcase that would work well, Shawn and Violet had gone back to Mesa Vecindad to finish packing. With Shawn's help, it hadn't taken long to get all of Violet's belongings packed up and stored in the trunk of Shawn's car. And since she had his help, her clothes weren't just haphazardly stuffed into the suitcase like she normally would have done.

Laughing at the good-natured teasing from him, she had allowed him to show her one of his packing tips. And giving him a hard time in return, Violet had put her hand on her hip and shook her head in amusement as he insisted that individually rolling each garment allowed for more space in the suitcase. When it was all said and done, Violet was still unconvinced that rolling was better than cramming when it came to fitting everything in. But her practical side caused her to admit that everything would arrive less wrinkled, and in the long run, that could save a lot of time.

With about an hour to spare once the packing was finished, they had decided to take a walk on the beach before meeting up with Shawn's source of information about Frank.

As they walked hand in hand, Violet thought to herself that being here with Shawn was far better than any other time she had walked these shores. She squeezed his hand and smiled up into his face when he turned to look at her.

"I'm glad you came here... even if you are a little headstrong." She laughed as he crinkled his nose.

"Hey now, isn't that a bit like the pot calling the kettle black?"

Violet stopped walking, which in turn caused Shawn to stop his long strides. Pulling him by the hand, Violet closed the gap between them and wrapped her arms around his stocky torso.

Breathing in his masculine scent, she sighed. "So, how are we going to work all this out anyway? I still want to be a missionary."

Shawn looked tired. And Violet wondered when he had developed the dark circles under his eyes.

"Let's just enjoy this moment before you start stirring things up again. Agreed?"

"Agreed. But you know we have to find a solution, don't you?"

"Of course. I wouldn't ask you to give up your dreams. But I was thinking that maybe you could volunteer at a mission in the States."

Violet squirmed out of Shawn's arms and started walking again. The idea of serving in the States was one he had brought up many times before, and the result was always an argument. But that was when she still had her heart set on being back here in Tijuana. Now, however, she wasn't so sure that Shawn's idea was a bad one. After being kidnapped, and now feeling haunted by the memories from that horrific event, Violet wasn't certain that serving in Tijuana was the best fit after all. Her time here had shown her how far reaching the effects of her past were and she had to admit that everything was different now.

She continued to walk as the thought worked its way through her mind. There were plenty of ministry opportunities in the States. If she decided to go that route, she would probably have a hard time deciding which one to serve at. She could choose from a wide variety: from serving in a crisis pregnancy center to ladling soup at a soup kitchen.

Smiling a bit, she realized that after serving at Mesa Vecindad, the idea of working a soup kitchen was actually appealing now. As she thought about her experience here in Tijuana, serving at the soup kitchen with Everest, she felt a stab of remorse. It seemed ridiculous now that she had ever felt that helping in a soup kitchen was somehow an inferior part of serving God.

Maybe that was what her time here in Tijuana was about. Maybe, along with learning to hate secrecy, she was supposed to learn how whatever you do for God is worthwhile and important.

She now began to understand that it doesn't matter whether you are the janitor cleaning the toilets or the pastor preaching a sermon, everything is needed and all those jobs work together to accomplish the same purpose. The key was to be where God wanted you to be so you could use your gifts and talents to their fullest.

Several verses flitted through her mind, causing her to smile as she remembered memorizing them in Sunday school as a small child. She smiled a bit more as she remembered how the words stumbled hesitantly out of her little mouth. She could almost hear her childish voice saying, "Colossians three, twenty-three: Whatever you do, work at it with all your heart, as working for the Lord..."

Feeling the heat of shame flare on her face, Violet acknowledged how that truth had been easy to forget, especially when she had allowed her pride to take control of her thoughts.

"You're right, Shawn."

Laughter exploded from Shawn as he said, "I don't think I heard you right! Can you say that again?"

"You're awful, you know that?" Violet punched him in the arm.

Shawn gave her the reaction she was hoping for. Reaching out his strong arms, he picked her up and slung her over his shoulder. She playful kicked and screamed in protest. How she had missed his playful flirting!

"Okay, in the ocean you go!"

"No! Shawn! I swear if you do, I'm taking you in with me!"

Shawn sprinted to the edge of the water, carrying her as if she was as light as a feather.

"I'll put you down on the sand if you give me a kiss!" He taunted.

"Are you kidding? I wouldn't kiss you now if you demanded it." She laughed as she punched him in the back. "Just put me down, you oaf!"

"That's it! This oaf is just going to have to show you who is boss." Shawn swung her down in a fluid motion, placing her feet in the surf. With teasing gruffness, he wrapped one of his large hands around her wrist, and then wrestled her other wrist into his hand as well. The fact that both her wrists were easily contained in just one of his hands made Violet feel small and vulnerable.

Keeping Violet from escaping his grip, Shawn placed his free hand behind her head and brought her lips to his. "Just shut up and kiss me!" he demanded in mock anger before he kissed her passionately.

The restrained possessiveness and hunger in his actions sent a tingle of fear up her spine. Not because of Shawn. No, he was harmless; he truly loved her and would never force himself upon her. But the fear that traced up her spine, sending panic to her heart, was because the situation felt too familiar.

It may have been over a year since she was held this way, but the memory rose in her mind with crystal clear detail.

In rapid succession, her mind replayed each terrible moment of her kidnapping. Suddenly, she no longer felt as if she were safe in Shawn's arms. Instead, she felt as if she had to flee for her life, she had to run from the emotions and memories that would leave her broken and trampled in their wake.

Bile rose in her throat and she started kicking at Shawn's legs.

Breaking the kiss, she said frantically, "Let me go! Let me go!"

Shawn immediately released her and took a few steps back. He held his hands up as if she were pointing a loaded weapon at him. Repentance and confusion battled behind his eyes, and the corners of his mouth were turned down and quivering.

Violet gasped for a calming breath, feeling sorry for the pain displayed on Shawn's face.

"Wh— what just happened there?" Shawn brought a shaking hand up to his head and ran it across his close cut red hair. "I thought we were flirting."

"It's nothing. I'm sorry." Violet couldn't stop her knees from shaking, so she sunk to the sand, sitting down.

"That's a lie. Something happened and you know it."

She couldn't look at him. Turning her gaze to the waves, she whispered, "The way you held me reminded me of... "

Shawn came and sat down next to her, slowly reaching out to her. His hand felt warm and calloused as it came to rest on top of her small, cold fingers. Turning her big, brown eyes to meet his blue ones, she blinked rapidly, refusing to let the tears fall. "It reminded me of... of the way he... he was so strong and I... I don't really know how I ever escaped him."

Violet didn't have to tell Shawn who she was talking about. Her fear made it obvious she was referring to the man who had kidnapped her.

"I'm sorry, Vi. I didn't know, you never... you never told me what he did to you. I'm sorry." He groaned in frustration.

"No. It's not you. Please, don't apologize. It's not about you, it's about... him. And how he... "Her words trailed off.

Shawn's face crumpled as he fought back tears. Bringing his hands to his face, he hid from her. "I could kill him... " he muttered through his hands. "God, help me, I have murder in my heart."

Seeing his reaction was her undoing. Pulling her knees to her chest, Violet tried to hide her face as well. Her pain— and guilt—were too great to be seen.

Feeling as if her chest would rip open if she held back her tears any longer, she let herself weep. For the first time since she had been kidnapped, she let go of the tight grip she had on her heart. Sobs took over her as pain from deep down in her soul spilled out.

But it wasn't just the pain from her kidnapping that flowed out through her sobs, it was every hurt she had ever felt.

For years and years, Violet had kept her emotions in check, never allowing others to fully see what she felt; afraid that somehow her emotions would grow too big for her to handle. It was easier to deny that she felt anything at all than to deal with the conflicting desires in her heart.

But as she sat next to her weeping fiancé, a tidal wave of grief swelled and erupted from her. Violet felt powerless to stop it, and as she was swept away she began to see it for what it was. Healing.

Years of bitterness toward Vivian were washed from her heart. And along with it went the overwhelming need to control her circumstances. Her control was little more than an effort to be better than her wayward sister, and it felt wonderful to admit that. It felt wonderful to let it go.

Sob after sob, unresolved hurt after unresolved hurt, Violet's heart broke free from the wall she had so carefully constructed around it. In one fell swoop, it was gone.

"Get it out, Vi. Just cry, let the tears heal you." Shawn was rubbing her back. His own tears trailing unchecked down his face.

Uncertain of how long she cried, she finally took a shaky, deep breath. Lifting her head, she wiped her eyes. "It happened, I can't deny it. But I'm here now, with you."

"Yes, yes you are. And you are safe with me." Shawn reached out and tenderly tucked a strand of blonde hair behind her ear, then wiped at the tears on her face. "And when you're ready, you can tell me all about it. You need to. But for now, just let God work His healing in you."

"I know." Violet nestled into his arms.

He began to hum a song and she marveled at how he seemed to know exactly how to soothe her soul. He was a steady rock for her to lean on.

"Shawn, I think I can face anything in this life, just as long as you are with me."

Chapter 25

The intense emotions had left Violet physically exhausted. She had been carrying a weight far too heavy to bear alone, and for far too long. And now that the burden was being removed from her shoulders, she marveled at how she had ever carried it, or why she had allowed herself to pick up that burden in the first place

As Shawn held her in his arms, she felt sweet relief. This man, who was content to simply hum and offer his support, was a God-send. His desire to protect her might be a bit aggressive sometimes, but it was just evidence of how fiercely he loved her.

Feeling secure and safe in his love, Violet drifted off to sleep without even knowing it would happen.

When she woke to his husky voice rumbling in his chest beneath her, she felt a moment of confusion. "Hmmm? What did you say?"

Kissing the top of her head, he said "I would be content to stay like this indefinitely, but we have to go. We're already late."

Rushing to her feet, Violet looked at the sky as if she could see the time written in the clouds. Shawn rose to his feet as well, and Violet felt a little self-conscious. *How long did I sleep?*

"Oh, no! I'm so sorry!"

Taking a step closer to her, Shawn leaned in and nuzzled her cheek with his nose. "Don't be. I held a beautiful woman in my arms while she slept, you'll hear no complaints from me."

Turning her face to receive his romantic touch, she said, "You should have woken me earlier. How long did I sleep?"

"Long enough for me to want to marry you... today. Let's not wait any longer."

Laughter bubbled up from Violet's heart. Not laughter born from jesting or a well delivered joke, but laughter from pure joy. "Your whispers of sweet nothings are only going to make us later than we already are."

"Violet, I mean it. Let's go today. Let's go back to the States and find a justice of the peace and get married."

"Don't tempt me." Her lips were almost touching his. "So, why the rush? I thought you wanted to stay here and find Frank Mr.-ruin-everyone's-life Smith."

"That's just it. I don't want Frank to ruin our lives. I've had a lot of time to think about everything. Our time apart has been good for me. I want to pursue you as energetically as I pursue justice. In my effort to protect, I don't want to neglect."

His words thrilled her. She had often wondered if he was a workaholic. "That's the most romantic thing you've ever said to me, Officer Sinclair."

"Ah yes, the ever-practical woman prefers boring statements over flowery words of flattery."

A pang of remorse slammed into her heart as she acknowledged how that hadn't always been the truth. *How I wish I hadn't let Santiago's sweet words work their flattery on me...*

Violet took Shawn's hand and pulled him away from the beach. Leading him to the broken concrete that was supposed to be a sidewalk, she reminded him of why he was there. "I would love to marry you today. But I don't want to be the one who distracts you from what you are called to do, and right now we better hurry up and go get some info on Frank.

"Okay. But you're not changing your mind. Just as soon as I meet up with my contact, I'm going to persuade you to find a justice of the peace... " Shawn started walking at a purposeful, rapid rate, pulling Violet along with him.

"You won't have to work very hard to persuade me. I'm eager to be your wife, your helper, your cheerleader. You are strong, smart, wonderful, and God-led. I believe in you, I trust you. And most of all, I love you."

Shawn stopped walking and turned to her. His whole face evidence of the power her words had on him. "And that, Miss Thompson, is something I could get used to hearing."

"Let's go!" Violet laughed. "You're so mushy right now!"

"What can I say? I'm in love with the most wonderful woman in the world."

· ◦ ●◉● ◦ ·

The restaurant where Shawn was to meet his friend was not much more than a hole in the wall. If she were just walking by on the street, Violet would never have had a desire to enter the establishment. The front window was covered in a film of dirt and grime. And the sidewalk in front was littered with broken bottles and various other pieces of trash.

However, the aroma that wafted out the open door spoke of delicious food.

Shawn slowed his step and placed a hand on the small of Violet's back, allowing her to step into the restaurant first.

It took a moment for Violet's eyes to adjust. The room was dimly lit and the contrast from the sun outside left her hesitant to keep walking.

Shawn seemed to be struggling to see as well. He squinted as he looked around. "Okay. We are definitely late, so he should be already seated and waiting for us."

Violet began looking around, too, even though she didn't know who they were looking for.

As her eyes scanned the restaurant, she noticed things like the ripped fabric in the seat of one of the booths, and how the carpet was threadbare and crusted with food in places. Most of the people eating there had a bottle of cerveza or a margarita sitting on their table.

Choking on the cigarette smoke that hung like a heavy fog in the air, Violet coughed into her hand. Trying to wave away the smoke, she turned toward the open door for some fresh air.

Suddenly, Violet's attempt to stop coughing changed to simply trying to breathe.

There, tucked in a side corner booth by the door, sat one of the men she had hoped to never see again. *Is this how Misty felt every time she had looked at the man who had kidnapped her?*

Feeling as if her feet were nailed to the floor, Violet was unable to move. Standing there, gaping at the man who had haunted her dreams, Violet felt the world begin to spin. As she reached behind her for Shawn, the man in the corner booth looked up.

As he stared into Violet's terror filled eyes, she knew he recognized her.

Chapter 26

December 1992

The day was warm and sunny, striking a contrast to the feelings in her heart. Unlike the sun in the clear blue sky, Violet's heart felt as if it were shrouded by cold, dark clouds of doubt. And fear.

Her time at The Mission had come to an end and Pastor Paul was taking her to the airport soon. She should be saying goodbye to all the dear children at the orphanage right now. But instead of spending her last few hours in Tijuana at The Mission, Violet had slipped away unnoticed.

By carefully coordinating each move she had made this morning, she had packed her things quickly, making sure she had enough time to accomplish the most important task of her life.

Now that she sat waiting for Misty to join her at the designated place, each moment seemed to take twice as long as normal.

Sitting on the graffiti laden bench at Playa Del Sol, Violet couldn't help but question her plan of action for the day. The antique brown and yellow striped suitcase sat a little bit away from her, filling her with feelings of nostalgia.

That suitcase represented so much. The very reason she owned it was because of Misty. Had Violet not needed an excuse to pick up the note Misty had dropped for her, the suitcase would most likely still be on display in the little tourist shop. The piece of luggage had been the perfect excuse for Violet to walk across that street to the place where the tattered piece of paper lay, waiting for her to read its message. And because of that, the suitcase represented the moment of truth when Violet knew she had to do something.

But it also represented the future—for both Misty and Violet. What Violet was about to do today would be life changing for Misty. But it would also be life changing for herself. If she could successfully pull off what they had planned, she would be part of something great. It was the kind of thing a person would want to share with the whole world, but Violet knew the only way for Misty to truly have the freedom she deserved was for Violet to never tell a soul.

If one word was carried to the man who claimed ownership of Misty, then it would all be over. He would go searching for her, and when he found her, there was no telling what he would do.

And so, she knew the action she was about to take would leave her unable to speak about the details of today to anyone. However, since everyone would think she simply slipped out to see Playa Del Sol one last time, the secret would be an easy one to keep.

For the thousandth time since agreeing on the plan, Violet whispered a desperate prayer. *God, please let this work.* Feeling anxious, Violet stood and looked around, hoping to catch a glimpse of Misty approaching. But there was no sign of her. Violet looked at the watch on her wrist. Misty was running late. *What is taking her so long?*

In an effort to look more relaxed, and therefore feel more relaxed, Violet untied her bright green tennis shoes and plunged her bare feet into the sand. A smile flickered across her face as she thought about what her mom would say if she knew Violet was wearing her shoes without socks. For years, her mother had tried to break her of the habit, but she had never succeeded.

Tossing her shoes aside, Violet sat down next to the suitcase. The long scarf she wore flapped in the breeze and she grabbed at it to keep it in place. She didn't want anyone to see her face; if she could remain anonymous, everything would go better.

The last time Misty and Violet saw each other, they had swapped clothing. Misty was to come to Playa Del Sol today dressed in Violet's clothes, and Violet, likewise was wearing the clothes Misty had given her, including the brightly colored scarf she struggled to keep in place.

After what seemed like an eternity, Misty finally came and sat near Violet. It seemed odd to see someone else in her clothes, but they did make the young girl look like a different person.

"Did you bring it?" Misty whispered.

"It's all in here," Violet patted the suitcase. "You've got a decent amount of cash, it should last you until you find a job." Obtaining the money had not been easy, but with a lot of prayer and a little creativity, Violet had been able to convince one of the local shops to cash a check for her. It had cost dearly, but it had worked.

"There's also a list of women's shelters in the States. Oh, and I got you a bus ticket for Portland, Oregon. There are directions to the bus station with all the other papers. Once you get to Portland you can decide where you want to go from there."

Misty's eyes filled with tears as she listened to Violet list off all the things in the suitcase. "You've been so kind to help me. You've thought of everything."

"I'm only doing what any other person would do. You came to me for help, how could I do anything else?"

"You have no idea, Violet... no idea. People look at me as if I am less than human. The disdain, disgust..."

"Don't you worry about all that. Where you are going, no one will know. And, please, don't ever let people make you feel as if you are the one to blame in all this. You had no choice. Those men are the ones who should be disdained." Violet reached out and rubbed Misty's shoulder. "Back to the details: I also put my passport in there. If you can get away with not using it, that would be great. I would rather not commit a crime if I don't have to. But, the last thing we need is for you to be stuck at the border and not able to pass through into the States. I've also listed my address, so please send the passport back to me once you've entered the States. If for some reason it gets lost in the mail, I can always report it as lost or stolen."

Violet took a few minutes to drill Misty concerning the information she would need to know to temporarily pass as Violet. Parting with her passport had been a tough choice, but Violet felt it a necessary action.

"Don't forget that from now until you reach Portland, you are Violet Thompson."

Misty nodded. "Then once I get there, I'm going to change my name."

"What?"

"I cannot stand who I am anymore. My whole life has been one search for a place to call home after another. And just when I finally felt I had arrived home, he was torn from me and killed. Right in front of me... as if karma or fate is punishing me. But the problem is... I don't know what I did to deserve being punished."

Without any adequate words, Violet simply shook her head in response. She started to argue that Misty was not being punished, that life was just unfair and didn't make sense sometimes. She wanted Misty to know that no matter what it felt like, God was there and He loved with intense, unconditional love. But Misty waved her hand at Violet in an action of dismissal and kept talking. She wasn't ready to hear about God.

"So, I'm going to give myself a new name to go with my new identity. I've been thinking long and hard about it, and well, I think I want my name to be Mercy." Scooting in the sand, Misty pulled Violet into a fierce hug. "If you hadn't shown me mercy, I would probably be dead right now, either from the hands of my pimp or from my own doing."

Shaking her head as the tears rolled down, Violet felt the truth of Misty's words deep in her heart. "I love it. You look like a Mercy. What about your last name?"

"Taylor." The word came out on a sob. "My husband's name was Taylor. I can't take his last name without raising the chances of them finding me, but I want to take his first name."

"It fits perfectly. And the risk shouldn't be too great."

Misty nodded. She released Violet from her grip and stood. "He'll think you are me. This will work. By the time he finds you at the jewelry store, I will be far away from here. When you take the scarf off, he'll see you're not me and then he will be left to wonder where I went."

"It will work. He'll find me instead of you. And by the time he starts looking for you, you'll have vanished, never to be found."

Misty was just bending to pick up the suitcase when a curse escaped her trembling lips.

Violet turned to see what Misty saw. Scanning the street, Violet was puzzled. She didn't see anything other than a single vehicle several blocks away.

"That's him. I would recognize that car anywhere. He's come looking for me, that... that... he's ruined our plan! It's like he knew! What do we do?"

Panicked, Violet shoved her feet into her shoes, not taking the time to tie them. "Go. Now. You have to go. This will still work, just run and don't look back!"

Misty pulled the suitcase up from the sand and looked to Violet one last time. "If I believed in God, I would say He sent you to me."

"He did. And He is with you as you find a new life."

With that, the girls turned and ran in opposite directions from each other. Misty ran toward the hope of freedom, while Violet ran toward the car that brought the man who had imprisoned Misty.

Violet was uncertain of what she should do, but one thing she knew for sure, Misty had to get away.

Chapter 27

Violet sprinted two full blocks before she slowed her pace. The desire to look back and make sure Misty was gone was strong, but she forced herself to keep her focus forward. Violet felt certain that anyone who looked at her would see fear pouring out, leaving an ugly trail. Her hands shook and her legs trembled, making it hard for her to walk. This situation was not what she had anticipated. The fact that this man was here looking for Misty showed Violet just how controlling he was. Misty hadn't been out of his sight for more than a half hour and he was already searching for her.

As the car came close, Violet kept her head down. She walked as if she had not seen or noticed it. But when they pulled up next to her and a man got out of the car, she had little choice about whether she would acknowledge him or not.

"Misty! What in the world are you doing here?" The man demanded, obviously angry. "You lied to me! You said you were going to buy some jewelry! But you never went there! What have you been doing?"

Violet looked up at the man through the scarf that hid most of her face. She had seen him several times before, but this was the first time she had seen him angry. His rage filled the air with an evil presence, making her desperate to run away. But the longer he stayed here, the farther Misty could run.

Not wanting to look into his eyes, Violet looked just past him. And as she did, her eyes met those of a young girl who was standing a mere thirty feet away.

The girl's eyes were large with fear and Violet willed her to run away. Why did she just stand there, watching as if she must see what would happen? For a moment, Violet felt she recognized the girl as the sister of one of Misty's friends.

But before she could figure out why she recognized the girl, Violet's attention was distracted from her as the man walked over to Violet. Cursing, he gruffly took hold of Violet's arm, wrenching it. Pain seared through her shoulder all the way to her fingertips and she cried out, terrified at how easily he could break her bone. There was no doubt it would be severely bruised.

"Worthless! That's what you are! I should show you right now how grateful you should be that I even waste my time on you!" Drawing back a fist in a display of power, the man threatened to strike Violet across the head.

Bracing herself for the blinding blow, Violet used her free arm to shield herself from him. As she raised her arm, she tipped her head back, causing the scarf to fall away from her face.

Shocked, the man let go of Violet's arm and dropped his fist. He was confused for a moment, shaken by the revelation.

"Where is she?" he yelled with frustration. "What have you done with her?"

Feeling emboldened by his reaction, Violet stood tall and straightened her shoulders. She looked him in the eye as the lie passed through her lips with ease. "I have no idea who you are talking about."

"Liar!"

Violet took a step back, putting distance between them. "Call me what you want. But I am not the woman you are looking for."

The man kicked at the ground in anger. Turning to the open window of the car, he spoke rapidly in Spanish to the man in the driver's seat, gesturing wildly.

Thinking this was her opportunity, Violet slowly took steps backward while keeping her eye on the man the whole time. In just a moment, she would be far enough away from him to make a run for it.

A few more steps, just a few more steps.

Suddenly, the man stopped talking and turned to look at her, apparently wanting to ask her something. With more cursing, he punched the car and yelled at her to stop.

Dizzying fear caused Violet to run as fast as she could. As the man ran after her, images of Misty and the women she worked with flashed through Violet's mind. If he caught her, she would probably be joining those girls—after she recovered from a beating. And most likely he'd find a way to get her to tell him where Misty went.

The plan had fallen to pieces. Regret sliced through her as she realized just how proud she had been to think she could handle this on her own.

Oh God, please help me!

Madly searching the street ahead for something to help her chance of escape, Violet slipped through an alleyway. Bursting out of the dark alleyway onto a busy street, Violet turned back to see how close the man behind her was, running blindly. It appeared as if she had lost him.

With a force that threated to knock the wind out of her lungs, Violet slammed into someone. The impact stopped her in her tracks and she struggled to keep her balance. Pushing herself away from the person, she glanced up to say she was sorry before she began running again.

Breathless and with a pain stabbing in her ribs, she felt helpless as a scream tore from her mouth.

Not only was she being chased by an angry pimp, now she was standing face to face with Santiago.

As he reached out to take hold of her, Violet willed herself to find another burst of adrenaline. Feeling faint, she tried to push at his hand.

"Let go, let me go!" she screamed.

Chapter 28

Ripping at Santiago's hands, Violet thrashed wildly in wide-eyed panic in an effort to free herself from the firm grip he had on her arms. Pain raced up the arm that had been wrenched, causing Violet to suck in a breath.

Just the sight of Santiago filled her with feelings so intense she felt her mind would explode. She had come to love this man. And now, instead of being in a relationship with him, feeling cherished and loved, she was fighting to be free of him. But she wasn't just fighting to be free from him; because of his lies and the people he associated with, she was certain that she was fighting for her very life. It seemed surreal, as if she were living out someone else's life. She had never thought something like this would happen to her.

Remembering all the reasons she had fallen in love with Santiago, Violet questioned how she had gotten to this point. Had he really been that good a liar? Or had she just been so blinded by her desire for love that she had refused to see him for what he really was?

But how would I have ever guessed he was a pimp looking for a new girl?

"I hate you!" She spat out the words. "I hate you, I hate you, I hate you!"

Watching to see his reaction, she saw his eyes narrow slightly before he turned to look to his left. And that's when she saw him. Santiago was not alone, and the man with him looked even more dangerous than the man who was looking for Misty.

"You know her?" the man asked Santiago with a wicked grin that exposed his many gold teeth. "Is she your next 'favorite'? I know how you like to have a favorite... hey, and lucky you, this one's free for the taking. You've paid some pretty high prices for your favorites before."

Santiago laughed as he motioned to the man, and said, "Keep her still for me Ricky. Don't let her get away."

With lightening quick reflexes, the man walked over to Violet. Standing behind her, he wrapped his strong, tattooed arms around her waist, pulling her tightly against his warm body. He smelled of cigarette smoke, cheap cologne and unwashed armpits.

The smells caused Violet to gag.

A flicker of what looked like compassion played across Santiago's face as he let go of her. Schooling his expression, he reached out to stroke her cheek. Even though Santiago was an evil man, the split-second evidence of emotion caused Violet to wonder if maybe he had loved her just a little—in a twisted, self-seeking sort of way.

But the fact that she was being held captive and forced to tolerate her body being pressed against that of such an unsavory man caused her to deny the possibility. Love would not allow her to be treated this way, no matter how twisted or perverted that love might be. The Santiago she knew would have rescued her from a situation like this, not create it. But apparently, the Santiago she knew did not exist.

Hating the feel of Santiago's fingers touching her cheek, Violet moved her head to the side. But when he simply laughed and roughly twisted her head upright, Violet felt outraged. She would not allow them to violate her, she would die first.

Blindly stomping her feet, she tried to smash the toes of the man holding her. She wriggled, arching her back, but the strength of the man was relentless. All her efforts just resulted in a tighter hold, leaving her feeling even more violated as the space between their bodies lessened. She now could feel the dampness of his perspiration soaking through her own clothing.

With admiration gleaming in his eyes, Santiago responded to Ricky's question. "She's a fighter, this one is. And you're right. This is definitely my new 'favorite.' I've had my eye on her for quite some time." Santiago leaned in close, bringing his lips to her forehead. "I almost had her convinced that she loved me, too. It would have been easier that way, but this will work."

He pulled back a little from Violet. A slight frown pulled down the corners of his mouth as he tipped his head just a bit to look at the man holding Violet. "But we both know that it's easy to make a woman think she's in love. Women will fall for any man that tells them they're beautiful. They're all looking for a knight in shining armor."

Violet could take no more. She wanted to cuss and scream. But neither of those could adequately express her disgust for him. Instead, she spit in his face.

Santiago wiped the saliva off his cheek, and then just looked at her, seething with anger.

"She's a feisty one, ain't she?" Ricky laughed, obviously amused.

As Ricky laughed, he loosened his grip on Violet enough that she was able to take a full step away from him even though his right fist still held her. Violet knew it was her opportunity to do something to get away. But all she could think about was how she wanted to hurt Santiago. Using every bit of energy she had, she kicked Santiago in the shin.

In response, Ricky pulled her back and held her so hard she wouldn't have been surprised to hear her bones breaking.

Reaching down to rub his leg, Santiago glared at her. Violet wondered if she had been foolish, while seeing his hurt made her feel slightly vindicated, she had to admit that she was extremely vulnerable.

As anger caused a vein to pulse in Santiago's neck, Violet realized that she may have just added one more thing to the list of stupid decisions she had made recently. But she had no way of knowing what would happen next because suddenly the man who was chasing her had found her.

"Santiago! You let go of her! She's mine." He yelled as he walked up to them.

Violet's fears about Santiago were confirmed at the words. They knew each other.

"No, she's mine, Jorge." Santiago wasn't intimidated, and Violet wondered if that should bother her. After all, Jorge was dangerous and pure evil. If Santiago wasn't afraid of him, then what did that make Santiago?

By running into Santiago, had she gone from the frying pan into the fire? "I don't belong to either of you! Let me go!"

"I'm not letting you just walk away. You know what happened to Misty. You have her scarf."

"The scarf is mine; I found it on the ground. I don't know what you are talking about! I have no idea who Misty is!" As the lies poured out of her, Violet wondered what Santiago was going to do. Was he just going to hand her over to this man?

It was obvious that Santiago knew better than to believe Violet didn't know Misty. She had been with Misty the last time she had seen Santiago. From the way she had acted, it was apparent that Misty knew Santiago. And to top it off, Misty was wearing the exact scarf that was loosely wrapped around Violet's neck right now.

Jorge moved to stand in front of Violet. "You're going to tell me where she went. She was my best girl. The men always paid top price for her." He yelled in her face, his hot breath moist on her skin.

The words made Violet's stomach churn. *How can they talk about women that way?*

Taking a few steps back, Jorge started to laugh, rapidly changing from anger to mocking. "You're just as pretty as Misty. With some make-up and better clothes, I bet you could earn a fair amount, too. So here's the deal, either you tell me where she is, or you take her place!"

"No! I'm not doing anything you say!" Violet wished Ricky would give her the freedom to slap the man.

"Shut up! I'm angry enough to beat you until you tell me where she is and then show you just what her life is like... right here! Stupid women like you need to learn their place and I'm an excellent teacher. I don't want to hear another sound out of you, you hear me? "

Jorge came toward Violet again and Ricky looked to Santiago as if asking what he should do.

Violet looked around the street for signs of possible help, but it was deserted. Still, she felt as if she should at least try to call for help, it was a long shot, but she had to take it. "Help! Somebody help me!"

As soon as she had shouted, Violet regretted it.

"I said shut up!" Without much warning, Jorge reached back his right arm to hit Violet.

Violet closed her eyes and braced herself, but the punch never made contact. Wilting against Ricky in relief, Violet almost cried when she saw that Santiago had stopped Jorge from hitting her.

Holding onto Jorge's wrist with his left hand, Santiago held up his right arm. His hand formed a fist and the threat didn't need words. "You aren't going to touch her. She's mine," he growled.

Jorge looked at Santiago for a moment. The tension between the men was thick. "What about Ricky?"

"What about him?"

Jorge turned and looked at the man in question. "He's never known to just hang around and help out without getting something in return. Why is he here with you?"

"That's none of your business, Jorge. You know how it works. You do your thing, I do mine. Maybe we just happened to be walking down the same street when this beauty ran into us."

Jorge relaxed his stance, "Okay. But she still knows where Misty went. The least you can do is make her tell me where she is."

"Frankly, I owe you nothing. And you know she doesn't know what happened to Misty, she's just a tourist. So get out of here, she's mine." Santiago's remark was flippantly bold.

Apparently it wasn't what Jorge wanted to hear.

In a moment blurred by fear and panic, Violet watched as Jorge lifted his shirt and pulled a gun out of the waistband of his pants. With a steady hand, he pointed it at Santiago.

"If she can't tell me where Misty went, then she stays. I'm not taking a loss."

Shaking the gun at Santiago like a scolding mother shaking her finger at a naughty child, Jorge asked, "So, have you changed your mind? Is the girl mine, or do I have to shoot you?"

Chapter 29

Santiago raised his hands. He seemed more annoyed than scared, and Violet marveled at how he could remain so calm when a crazy man was pointing a gun at him. She, on the other hand, could feel fright reverberating through her whole body.

Come on, Jorge, put the gun down," Santiago said calmly. "There's no need for that."

"I'm not joking with you, man. I need the money Misty brought in."

"But how do you know she's gone?"

"Stop playing games..." Jorge started shifting his weight from foot to foot, agitation making his movements stilted and quick. "Stop wasting time! She's gone. When a girl tells you she'll be somewhere and then she's not there when you go check up on her, you know she's run away. It happens."

"Not to me," Santiago smirked. "You must not be treating them right, Jorge."

Jorge swore before yelling, "Shut up!" Then he spun on his heels and pointed the gun at Violet's head. "Either she goes with me, or she goes with no one."

Violet bit her lip in an effort not to cry. If she started, she wondered if she would ever be able to stop. And since Jorge had demanded her silence, she was scared to see what reaction her crying would bring.

"Hey, hey, calm down there. You know you can't make any profit by killing the girl." Santiago took a step toward Jorge with his hands still raised. "How about we make a deal? I've been known to pay a handsome price when a woman strikes my fancy."

Jorge lowered the gun and looked at Santiago with interest.

Santiago nodded his head to his hip, "May I?"

When Jorge gave him permission, Santiago reached into the pocket of his pants and pulled out a large roll of bills. "If you give me the gun, I'll give you the cash and we can all be on our way."

Looking at Santiago with greed and a trace of suspicion gleaming in his eye, Jorge threw the gun a little past Santiago.

Tossing the money at Jorge's feet Santiago said, "That's more than enough."

Watching Jorge pick up the money, Violet couldn't believe what she saw taking place. Bile rose up in her throat and she choked on its acrid taste. Coughing, she gasped for air. *I've just been bought!*

"Come on Ricky, let's go," Santiago commanded as he bent to pick up the gun. He quickly tucked it into his own waistband.

Violet wasn't sure if she liked the idea of him having a gun. However, she knew he could easily kill her with just his hands, so gun or no gun, her life was still in danger. But since he did have the gun, and she knew where it was, maybe at some point she would be able to take it from him and use it for her escape.

As Ricky started dragging her along the street, Violet kicked her legs in protest. "My car is just around the corner, I can take you somewhere if you want. Might be easier than dragging her wherever you're taking her."

Santiago nodded in agreement then allowed Ricky to lead the way to the car. Uninvited, Jorge followed, counting the bills as he walked.

When they reached the car, Violet searched her mind for some kind of action she might take. If she got in that car, she might be taken so far from The Mission that she would never find her way back. She couldn't just let them do this. She wasn't a piece of furniture to be purchased. She was a person! But try as she may, other than getting her hands on that gun, she couldn't formulate a plausible plan. She was at their mercy. Her only hope was for God to intervene.

God, please! I was just trying to help Misty. Please, please save me!

Santiago opened the back passenger door and Ricky started to roughly push her in.

"Let's tie her up first," Santiago commanded. "Got any rope in your car?"

When Ricky handed her over to Santiago so he could go in search of a rope, Violet kicked and slapped and scratched, but one twist of her wounded arm and she was rendered limp. Each time the arm was handled, the pain was worse. This time, it was so great she almost blacked out. She sank to the ground and helplessly watched as Ricky handed Santiago a rope.

"There isn't nearly enough money here!" Jorge complained.

Santiago brushed off his comment with the wave of a hand.

Ricky bounded to the driver's seat as Santiago tightly bound Violet's wrists and shoved her into the car. With a resounding thud, he closed the door.

"I said that's not enough money!" Jorge grabbed Santiago by the shirt.

Instead of replying, Santiago threw a punch. Hitting Jorge square on the jaw, the man went flying backward, landing on his rear end. By the way he swayed, he was clearly stunned.

Santiago quickly opened the front passenger door and sat down as Ricky turned the key and brought the engine to life.

Fighting to stay conscious, Violet sat up and looked out the window. As the car took off, she could see Jorge running behind, screaming and yelling that Santiago had cheated him.

"Greedy pig," Santiago muttered. Turning to look at Ricky he said, "You can drop us off at the old warehouse; you know the one?"

"Yes, I do. But what are you going to do there?"

Santiago smiled, "Wouldn't you like to know…"

Chapter 30

As the car sped across bumpy residential roads, Violet began to recover from feeling faint. The pain in her arm was abating, causing her strength to return. Pulling against the ropes that bound her wrists, she struggled to free herself. With each twist and pull, the rope burned her skin. The intense stinging brought tears to her eyes, but it was the feelings of defeat that caused the tears to fall. Hating how they traced down her cheeks to drip off her chin, Violet pulled her face to her shoulder to wipe them away. But it was no use; one after the other, more tears fell in rapid succession.

This is stupid. I'm being taken against my will to some creepy warehouse so Santiago can do who knows what to me and all I do is sit here and cry?

Taking a deep, settling breath, Violet willed her tears to stop. She closed her eyes and took in several more ragged breaths, whispering desperate prayers with each exhale. When the tears fell less frequent, she told herself to get angry. Wallowing in pity would get her nowhere, but if she were to feel rage or indignation she would feel like fighting against Santiago and his plans. And in her mind, fighting would offer a greater chance of escape than crying.

Purposely, Violet recalled memory after memory of Santiago's sweet words of love. As the memories filled her mind, they also filled her with the outrage she was seeking.

I'm a stupid, stupid idiot! I walled up my heart for years only to tear it down and fall in love with a pimp!

By the time she had completely stopped her crying, fury burned inside her. "How dare you! What a sorry excuse for a man you are! I hate you, Santiago!" She screamed as loud as she could, the words feeling good as they passed through her lips.

Drawing her knees up to her chest, she put all her energy into kicking the back of Santiago's seat. She wasn't certain what she had expected from him: irritation, a yelled response, something to show his displeasure at her outburst. But just like his reaction to Jorge's threatening gun, Santiago was annoyingly calm. He merely turned his head to look at her and said, "Be quiet, Violet."

Ricky glanced at Santiago, mirth making his eyes sparkle. "You're gonna have some fun with this one! Nothing boring about her, that's for sure."

Santiago didn't respond. He just turned back to the window, staring at the scenery as it passed by.

Santiago's cool reaction, paired with Ricky's comment, fanned the flame of fury in Violet. "You said you loved me! You said you loved God! I hope you burn in hell for the lies you've told!" She ground the words out through gritted teeth, her anger made her voice sharp and cutting.

Santiago whipped his head to look at her. The wounded look in his eyes told her that her words had hit their mark. Something inside her thrilled to see that glimpse of pain as it flashed across his face, followed by a scowl of displeasure. It may have only been a split second, but it had been there, she'd seen it. "Oh, did you not like that? I'm sorry, but... like you've shown me today, the truth can be brutal."

Violet's mocking words echoed in the silent car. Santiago sighed, his jaw was set and his lips were in a tight line.

Ricky was trying to look at Violet and Santiago while he drove. He glanced between them while trying to keep an eye on the road.

The air seemed to almost crackle with the tension.

Violet laughed, "What's the...?"

"Shut up, Violet." Santiago growled interrupting whatever she would say next. "I should have taped your mouth shut."

"You think you can silence me?" Violet screeched in wild outrage. "You think you own me? Well, you have another think coming!" Violet took her tethered hands and punched at Santiago's head with both her fists. She wasn't much of a threat and he simply shifted in his seat to avoid the punches she threw. "You're the sorriest excuse for a man I have ever seen. You lie and cheat. You woo and speak words of love—empty words! All so you can destroy the very heart and soul of whomever strikes your fancy."

Violet's brown eyes were narrowed, brimming with tears. "You make me sick." She struck at him again.

"I said, shut up!" Santiago turned in his seat, and shouted at her. Frustration emanated from his body, causing his face to turn red. "Just shut up already and stop flapping around; you have no idea what you are talking about!"

"I do know what I'm talking about!" she shouted back. All common sense was long gone. She had wanted to be angry so she would fight for her life instead of just cry, but her rage had taken over. She was no longer fighting for her escape; she simply wanted to punish Santiago with her words. She wanted to hurt him like he had hurt her. "I know the truth and so do you. You're a man who lacks integrity, you have no honor. You deserve no respect."

Santiago sighed loudly, signaling the end of his patience. He turned to look at Ricky, "Why did we not gag her or something?"

Ricky raised his eyebrows and glanced at Santiago. "Just wait 'til you've shown her who's boss. She'll not be so bold then." Ricky gazed into the rearview mirror with open lust in his eyes. "I wouldn't mind putting her in her place if you need help."

"Just focus on getting us to the warehouse, the rest is none of your business." Santiago looked as if he would take his frustration out on Ricky. The glare that punctuated his words left Violet feeling more than a little nervous. Maybe she had pushed him too far.

Uncertain what she should do, Violet looked out the window and saw they were now on the outskirts of town. The buildings they passed were no longer private houses. The large buildings looked abandoned; weeds grew tall, graffiti marked the walls and most of the windows were broken out. Some of the openings were boarded up, while others were just gaping holes. The broken glass on the ground sparkled in the sunlight and Violet thought the big, pointy shards looked like weapons of torture just waiting to be used.

A shudder worked its way up Violet's spine. This would be the perfect place to film a horror movie.

Bile burned the back of her throat and Violet worried she would be sick.

This wasn't a film site. This was real life—this was her life.

Chapter 31

Remembering how both Ricky and Santiago were familiar with the old warehouse, Violet wondered what secrets the walls of the abandoned buildings kept. How many other women had been dragged out here against their will? And what had been done to them? The pain Violet had seen in Misty's eyes had spoken volumes about the trauma she had suffered at the hands of cruel men, and Violet desperately hoped she wouldn't have to personally know the injustices that happen to defenseless women.

When the car came to a stop, Violet's heart began to race even faster. It was now or never. If she didn't act now, her life was going to radically change; she was certain that every ounce of virtue she had treasured all her years was going to be stolen from her. She had to do something. She had to escape before that could happen.

"Just let us out and go on," Santiago ordered. The words stopped the frantic thoughts that were swirling in her mind. Santiago wanted it to be just them.

Maybe I can talk some sense into him. Maybe... but his next words stopped any hopeful thoughts she had. "I don't want a witness. What I'm going to do to her needs to remain unseen and unknown by anyone but her and me. But I guarantee," Santiago grinned, "what happens here will be something she'll never forget... nor will I."

Ricky laughed and his eyes danced with malice. "You make a fellow tempted to stay and watch. Maybe I could learn a thing or two from you on how to make a woman show the proper respect."

"There's no doubt you could learn more than just a thing or two from me," Santiago replied smugly. "But not today. Today, it's just me and my new favorite."

Santiago opened his door and stepped out of the car. Slamming his door shut, he quickly came to the rear passenger door and opened it to pull Violet out.

As soon as his hands reached toward her, Violet began kicking, hitting and spitting. Her damaged arm protested against her actions, but she was so terrified she barely noticed the pain.

Santiago cursed, telling her to calm down and to quit fighting him. The ugly word caused Violet to become still. She had no idea why, but the filthy word he'd used shocked her. It was so contradictory to the Santiago she knew and loved. And even though he had proven to her that he was not the man she had thought he was, the word still startled her.

Santiago took advantage of her calm. Reaching in, he grasped the rope around her wrist and heaved her out of the car.

Feeling her body being lifted off the seat brought her back to her senses and she began fighting him again. By the time he had her out of the car, she was dizzy from the pain zipping through her damaged arm and sitting on the ground at his feet, choking back sobs.

He slammed the door shut and motioned for Ricky to drive away.

Ricky didn't just slowly accelerate and pull away; instead, he stomped on the gas pedal. The tires spun and threw up dirt and gravel.

Violet was encompassed in a cloud of dirt, and it stuck to the trails her tears had left, leaving her face streaked with mud. Coughing and gagging on the dust that got in her mouth, she struggled against the rope that restricted her from effectively wiping the brown, gritty trails off her face. She was pitiful, heartbroken, and desperately praying for God to give her strength.

When Ricky's car disappeared, Santiago pulled Violet up from the ground and pressed her body against his. The action was hungry and needy, his hands hot on her skin. She could feel the steady thumping of his heartbeat and the quick rise and fall of his chest as he breathed heavily.

She stiffened and tried to push against him, but he just tightened the hold he had on her. "Don't fight me. Just let me kiss you."

She kept pushing against him as he buried one of his large hands in her hair. He pulled her head toward his and kissed her passionately.

The sensation of his lips on hers reminded Violet of the times they had kissed before. Shame filled her. She should never have let that protective wall be broken down by his words of love and false claims of being a man of God.

Struggling to fight off the pressing of Santiago's embrace, Violet cried out for him to untie her hands.

"Promise you won't run away?" he asked while his lips were pressed to her neck in a series of kisses.

Violet lied, promising to stay. She felt absolutely no remorse for lying; it was such a stupid question. Of course she was going to run; she'd be a fool not to.

As soon as her hands were free from the rope, Santiago grabbed her by the wrist and pulled her toward the warehouse. Every nerve in Violet's body tingled a warning. Swallowing her pride, she stepped closer to Santiago. She took her free hand and ran it down his arm. Turning to her with a surprised smile, he stopped walking.

Standing on her tip toes, she moved to kiss him. Wrapping her arms around him, she took fistfuls of the fabric at the back of his shirt.

Santiago responded to her touch and was lost in the moment. He was so focused on kissing her, he never even felt her hands pull Jorge's gun from his waistband.

Desperate to escape, Violet pushed the barrel of the gun against Santiago's chest. His face registered surprise as he took a step back, his hands loose at his sides. Without any warning, Violet smashed the gun across his head. The sound of metal smashing against his skin was sickening, making her shudder with disgust.

The blow left Santiago stunned. He swayed just a bit as he took a steadying step toward her.

With quick, determined movements, Violet bashed his head with the gun again. This time, there was a distinctive crack as the weapon slammed against his skull. The gun slipped from her grasp and went flying, landing with a clatter amongst the broken shards of glass.

Santiago sank to his knees as blood poured out from his head. "Violeta?" he whispered tenderly as if he were the man who had wooed her on the beach.

The word stopped her heart. She used to thrill at the sound of her name tumbling out of his mouth in Spanish.

Violet's heart sank as she realized the most practical thing would be to shoot him. But try as she may, she couldn't bring herself to even think about pulling the trigger. Afraid he would rouse enough to rise and get the gun, Violet turned to go looking for the weapon.

"Violeta," Santiago mumbled. "You must stay with me."

Anger filled Violet and she stopped mid-step. Did he think she was an idiot? She wasn't going to fall for his empty sweet talk again. Turning around, she ran up to him, giving way to the rage that superseded all common sense. With much more force than she thought possible, she kicked him in the chest. The impact knocked him backwards causing him to hit his head on the side of the warehouse, her kick stealing the air from his lungs.

Violet retrieved the gun. Then she ran. As she ran she could hear Santiago's struggle to fill his lungs with air again. The strangled coughing echoed through the abandoned warehouse, warning Violet that she didn't have much time until he would pursue her.

I should have shot him.

Chapter 32

She was running without a clue where she was going. Nothing looked familiar and she wondered if she would ever find The Mission.

Violet's pulse pounded in her veins, and her feet were pounding on the ground. With all the events of the last few weeks swirling in her head, Violet tried to focus on the two main things—the fact that she was alive and free, and the fact that she needed to keep running to insure she would remain alive and free.

The reality that she had been kidnapped was something she couldn't process right now; it was something she might not ever be fully able to work through.

Just this morning, as she set her plans in motion, it hadn't seemed possible that things would have taken such a dangerous turn. Yet, if she looked past the surface, Violet knew she would see all the warning signs. It had been a very poorly constructed plan. She shouldn't have been so naïve in thinking she didn't need help in rescuing Misty. *How could I have been so stupid?*

With each panicked step, Violet had to force herself not to look back. Was she being followed? What if she were caught? The exertion of running had exhausted her and she knew her chances of fighting off another attack were pitiful. It had been hard enough to free herself from Santiago's strong arms the first time—even with the fresh burst of adrenaline. Now, however, her adrenaline was wearing off, and shock was setting in. Her teeth were chattering and she was freezing cold, even as she felt the sweat beading up on her forehead.

Seeing a familiar street, Violet felt renewed strength surge through her.

I just have to get to The Mission... just a little farther... The Mission... then I'll be okay.

Suddenly, Violet was aware of a ticking sound. Fear raced down the back of her neck as she imagined all sorts of different things that could be making the sound. Keys jangling in one of her captor's pockets as he ran after her? Or was it bullets in his pocket? Was she going to be shot?

She had no way of knowing exactly who might be chasing her, and who was responsible for the sound she was trying to identify. It was possible that Jorge was still seeking to make up for his loss of Misty by making Violet take her place. Had he been waiting in the shadows, hoping she would escape Santiago?

When Violet found herself sprawling toward the ground, she tried to make the impact of the street be on her hands instead of her head. But the action was too late, and with a muffled cry, she landed flat on her face. Stunned, she lay there for a second trying to breathe, mentally taking inventory to see what was hurt.

Am I shot? Is that what happened?

Thankfully, the only searing pain she felt was in her already damaged arm. With a sigh of relief, she realized she hadn't heard the bang of a gunshot, either. Rolling to her side, Violet tried to push herself up with her good arm. Gasping in agony, she quickly realized that even though her face had taken the brunt of the impact, she had hurt her wrist as she tried to break her fall- now both of her arms suffered injury.

Her second try was successful and as Violet sat up, she saw that she was missing a shoe. Gingerly touching her already swelling eye, she saw the bright green shoe a few feet away from her. In her panic to get away, she had forgotten that her shoes were untied. And apparently, the untied laces had been lashing against the street, making the sound she had heard — until she had tripped herself on them. The fact that she would do something as impractical as running with untied shoes bothered her.

Just one more thing to prove my stupidity.

Fearing the fall had cost her precious time, Violet jumped to her feet and started running. She didn't stop to retrieve the shoe that had come off. She was too scared and too dazed from the blow to her head to care. All she could think about was getting away from it all. She had to get away from Santiago and Jorge. It might even be possible that

Ricky was chasing her; the lecherous look in his eyes had confirmed his lust to dominate her.

Trying to gather the pieces of her broken heart while she ran, she thanked God that she had kept her purity intact. Even though she had lost a lot of innocence today, things could have been far worse.

Even so, she knew that no one could ever know what had happened. If anyone ever found out, the ramifications would be too great. Misty could be found. The Mission would be a target for crime due to her connections there. And her own dreams of being a missionary to Mexico would be demolished; no one would want someone so tangled in danger to be involved in their ministry. She had to move on, she had to recover. She had to dispose of the gun that she held in her hands. But most of all, she had to protect her secret.

I have to get home… no one can know what I did to deserve this. I should have asked for help with Misty…

Giant tears of shame and remorse rolled from her eyes as she ran. *I should have known better than to fall in love.*

Chapter 33

April 1994

Violet desperately grabbed for Shawn's hand. She needed to know he was there, standing behind her. She needed to feel his strong hand grasping hers, reminding her that she wasn't alone to face this man who dominated her nightmares.

Backing up, Violet bumped into Shawn while still holding the gaze of the man sitting in the corner booth. She acutely felt the desire to escape, but she couldn't seem to tear her eyes from his. She had an urgent need to turn around and run out of the seedy little restaurant, but her feet were firmly planted in place.

Violet's arm began to throb as if she were still suffering the physical harm that had come to her the last time she had seen the strong, intimidating man who was looking at her so intently.

Confused and panicked, Violet felt as if time had been altered. Every action appeared to be in slow motion—from her own breathing to the movements of the man scooting out of the booth to stand. But her mind, however, felt as if it were racing faster than normal.

For with each step the man took toward her, it seemed Violet remembered a dozen things she had tried to forget about him. He may have only walked halfway from the booth to her, but in the time it took him to walk those six steps she had already re-lived that terrible day.

Shawn, who was standing closely behind her, held one of her cold, yet sweaty hands while resting his other hand on her shoulder in an intimate gesture. He seemed unaware of the trauma and panic she was experiencing. Instead, he seemed relaxed as he softly said, "There he is!"

Stunned, Violet turned her head and looked at Shawn to see if he was looking in the direction she thought he was. Sure enough, he was looking at the man walking toward her.

Nothing made sense. Try as she might, Violet could not understand why Shawn appeared to recognize the dangerous man she needed to escape from.

When the man came close enough, he searched Violet's face with his eyes before he spoke.

"Violeta?" her name was whispered in disbelief, as if he were just as surprised to see her as she was to see him.

The fluid sound of his voice brought to the surface a myriad of emotions that Violet had tried to forget. And as they poured over her, her ears began to ring as an inky black cloud inched its way around the edges of her sight. With fluttering eyelids, Violet's knees gave out. Had it not been for Shawn standing behind her, she would have fallen to the floor. But instead, she was suspended in Shawn's strong arms and pulled close to his chest in a protective manner.

"Violet? Are you ok?" Shawn's voice was calm, yet Violet knew him well enough to hear the alarm he tried to mask. He turned to Santiago with a look of confusion.

"He... no! Don't let... " Violet was unable to speak a complete sentence as she struggled to fight off the dark cloud descending on her. Hating the helpless feeling of being lightheaded, Violet willed herself to stay conscious. Now was not the time to be weak or faint.

Shawn gently shook her and she roused fully. Without being able to take her eyes off of him, she watched Santiago walk back to his booth, and deftly retrieve a glass of water.

He's so muscular. And handsome... and dangerous.

She spun around and clung to Shawn's shirt, pulling him closer to her so he could hear her broken whisper. "Get me away from him."

"Who?" Shawn glanced around the room as if looking to see who she was talking about. "Who are you scared of?"

Violet didn't have time to answer before Santiago stood before them, offering Violet the glass of water. "Violeta, turn around and take a sip," he commanded. The authoritative tone in his voice irked Violet. How dare he tell her what to do?

Spinning to face Santiago, Violet reached out for the water. Taking the glass from his hand, she quickly flicked her wrist, sending the water spraying. Santiago gasped and flinched as the cold water saturated his face, as well as the front of his shirt.

Shawn was still holding on to Violet's waist, and she pulled against his strong grip. It felt too familiar, standing here in front of Santiago again, being held by strong arms.

"Violet! What are you doing?" Shawn asked in disbelief. Her action had shocked him.

Drying his face, Santiago laughed. It was a laugh that lit up his eyes and filled his face with joy. There was no trace of anger in his voice as he said, "I guess I completely deserved that!"

Shawn let go of Violet and shifted his weight to look at Santiago. His eyes were large and his forehead was creased in puzzlement. "What is going on here? Santiago, do you know my fiancée, Violet?"

"Fiancée? Congratulations, Shawn, but watch out, she might break your heart," Santiago said as he continued to laugh. The sound grated on Violet's nerves. She narrowed her eyes, straightened her shoulders and leveled her gaze on Santiago while she answered the question Shawn had asked Santiago. "Yes, he knows me. And at one time I thought I knew him." She turned away from Santiago and added, "But now I wish I had never known he existed." Her words were cold and emotionless.

"Actually, if I may correct you," Santiago spoke with no ire, just the same calm he always possessed. "You did know me. But then you were too scared to see the truth, and so you ran. I'm wondering, Violeta, do you often run from your troubles without gathering all the knowledge you need?"

His words stung as much as if he'd slapped her in the face.

Shawn sighed as he brought a hand up and drew it across his face. He was unable to follow the conversation; Violet could see his frustration as plain as day. "Can someone please fill me in? It's obvious that you two know each other and that I have no idea what you are talking about."

Santiago raised an eyebrow and stared at Violet, waiting for her to explain. She had had enough of his cocky, cool exterior. He always acted as if he were in complete control. It had been a character trait of his that had attracted her to him, but not now. He had proven himself untrustworthy, and if she couldn't trust him, she certainly didn't want him in control.

"He's the man who kidnapped me." Violet blurted out and took a step toward Shawn. When he opened his arms, she walked into Shawn's comforting embrace. "He kidnapped me," she declared again as a shiver caused her to shudder. Her voice sounded small and frightened.

Shawn's face instantly turned scarlet, matching his fiery red hair. Pivoting in place, he held Violet safe in the circle of his strong arms and glared at Santiago. "What did you do?" Shawn snarled with barely controlled rage. Then he quietly growled, "What did you do? I'll punch your face in... So help me, I'll kill you."

Santiago took a step back and lifted his hands in a gesture of peace. "Shawn, you know me. You've known me for years. I would never hurt anyone. Especially Violet."

"What do you mean? 'Especially Violet?'" Shawn looked at Santiago with suspicion.

"It means that we had been dating before I found out his secrets." As the words fell from her lips, Violet felt heartbroken and embarrassed at the same time.

Santiago shook his head. "No. It means that I loved you more than life itself… " He hesitated, staring into her eyes with vulnerability. Then he spoke in a barely audible voice, "I still do."

Chapter 34

The force of his words slammed into Violet's chest, leaving her feeling as if she had been punched. "How dare you? How dare you start those manipulative lies again?"

Pain was etched in her face as she looked from Santiago to Shawn—one man was filled with rage and jealousy while the other looked broken and defeated. Of course, Shawn was angry, but what confused her was Santiago. Why was he acting the way he was?

It didn't seem fair, just when life had been starting to make sense, that this had to happen. Why couldn't she just walk away from the past and begin her future? "You need to leave this restaurant and leave us alone, Santiago. I never want to see you again—ever."

"Violeta, I can't just walk away, I'm here to talk with Shawn. I'm his lead, his contact."

Violet brought her hands up to cover her face. She couldn't do this; she couldn't stand here and hold a conversation with the man who had purchased her to be his new favorite. She should be running away from him or hurting him—anything other than what was going on right now. And how was it possible that he was here to talk to Shawn? Was Shawn just as corrupt as Santiago? Did he have secrets he was hiding, too?

"Unless you explain things to me, there is no way I'm going to talk to you, Santiago." As Shawn bit off the words, Violet's heart soared and she knew it had been foolish to question Shawn's integrity.

"She says you kidnapped her, and you say you love her. Call me stupid, but something doesn't add up." Taking an agitated step toward Santiago with his fists clenched at his sides, Shawn continued, "I may know you and call you 'friend,' but I know Violet better. So it's in your best interest to start explaining things before I stop restraining myself."

Shawn opened and closed his hands, drawing attention to his fists. "I promise you, all it would take is one word from her that you did anything—I mean anything—to harm her, and I will mete out my own justice right here, right now."

"I understand why you're upset." Santiago spoke the contrite words with complete conviction. "All I can do is tell you what I know, then it's up to you and Violet whether you believe me or not." He looked first at Shawn, but then he turned to Violet with his heart in his eyes. "Violeta, I would never hurt you and I never lied to you. I did not kidnap you; I rescued you. I removed you from a very volatile and dangerous situation. You were just too scared to see what was happening."

"But you tormented me as you forced me into the car, you tied my hands while you cussed at me. You pushed me around and didn't care that my arm was broken." Disgust and torment warred for dominance in the tone of her voice, "You bought me and told Jorge I was to be your new favorite; that I was just one woman in a long list of other women who you've purchased. And then you forced your kisses on me!"

"Whoa, wait a minute! How did he buy you? What in the world are you talking about?" Shawn's eyes were large. As his mind worked through the limited information he was hearing, he grew more confused and angry. "Is this why you never talked about your last trip to Mexico? Were you?... did?... he... " Shawn stumbled on his own conclusion, unable to formulate the questions running through his mind. "He bought you from a pimp? Santiago rescued you from working the streets?"

"No!" Both Santiago and Violet whispered insistently at the same time.

"I was helping a girl run away from her pimp. Things didn't go as planned and I was running away from the man when I bumped into Santiago. And that's when he paid the man... that's when he bought me, like he's done with other women he took a fancy to. That's when I learned that our dating relationship was nothing more than a trap; he was wooing me simply so he could use me. And when I didn't go along with it, he simply bought me."

Rolling his eyes in exasperation, Santiago said, "I didn't buy you to be my new favorite like I told Jorge, I purchased your freedom. I paid the ransom for your life. Can't you see that?"

Violet swallowed hard as tears rushed to her eyes. It made sense. It made much more sense than the idea that Santiago was a corrupt, wicked man. "If what you claim is true, then who were the other women that Ricky and Jorge were talking about?"

"I bought their freedom, too." Tears rolled untouched down Santiago's face. "I would never harm you, Violeta. I only did what I had to. I couldn't let them know I loved you, and for the safety of every other woman I have ever helped, I couldn't let them know my real identity. I really was working in law enforcement like I told you. It's a long story and I don't have time to tell it all; but basically, I was working as a police detective. Then, when I saw so much injustice, I had to do something to help. And so I did the only thing I could. I used the resources I had to bring about the change I had begged God to give these women."

Shawn's expression was unreadable as he walked over to a table and flung himself into a chair. Violet followed him, uncertain what she was supposed to do. Soon, Santiago joined them at the table and they sat in stunned silence for a few minutes.

With a raspy, emotion-filled whisper Shawn broke the silence. "Thank you. For saving Violet's life. And for daring to save the lives of others."

Santiago looked uncomfortable with the expression of gratitude. He simply shrugged his shoulders and looked down at his hands that were clasped on the tabletop.

"The money... where did it come from?" Violet's voice trembled. She tentatively reached out her hand to touch his. "I'm sorry I doubted you. I said horrible things."

Again, Santiago shrugged in discomfort, pink stained his cheeks in embarrassed humility. "The money came from my late parents' estate. God blessed me with the inheritance and so I used that blessing to purchase the freedom of those who desire it."

Shawn's gaze was riveted on Violet's hand grasping Santiago's. His displeasure caused Violet to feel a pang of guilt and she quickly withdrew her hand, placing it in her lap. With Santiago's confession of his innocence, her feelings toward him had taken a huge shift. With dismay, Violet realized she was sitting at a table with two men she loved. At some point she would have to decide which one she loved more and who she wanted to be with. But right now, she needed more information.

"So the warehouse, you took your 'favorites' there and then just let them walk away?"

"Oh, Violeta, it's just not that simple. Freedom from sex-trafficking is so complicated and dangerous. That's why you should have asked for help instead of trying to rescue Misty on your own. Wearing her clothes and fooling her pimp was foolhardy, so, so foolhardy. I just thank the Lord that He put me where I was that day."

They sat and talked for a while, each filling in the gaps and their parts of the story until all three of them had a better understanding of the situation. As the story unraveled, they each expressed gratitude at how everything had turned out. While things had not been handled as well as they could have, God, in His infinite mercy and grace, had worked past their mistakes. But they were all worried for Misty. It had been over a year and no one had heard from her. Before Violet had gotten involved, Santiago had decided that Misty would be his next target for rescuing. He had even lined up someone in the States to help her heal emotionally and help her be ready to live a new life of freedom. The fact that Misty had simply fled Mexico for the States without those vital stays in a transitional half- way home being her destination caused Santiago to fear Misty would fall back into the trafficking.

Even though Violet's passport had been returned, there had been no note or anything to indicate where Misty was headed. The postmark was Portland, Oregon, but that was to be expected since Violet had purchased a ticket to that city for Misty.

Had Violet been able to go back in time, there were many things she would have done differently in her attempt to help Misty; loaning her passport was one of them. Violet had never broken the law before, and even though it seemed justified at the time, she knew it had not been the right thing to do.

"We need to track her down," Violet said, trying to push past the guilt she felt over the passport. "I need to know she's safe."

"I agree. But right now, I need to talk to Santiago about Frank Smith. That's why I'm here after all. He's out there, and as long as he's on the loose, I feel Rachel is still in danger. Maybe even you, Violet, since you two girls are so close."

Santiago closed his eyes in weariness; their conversation kept moving from one heavy topic to another. "Frank is here in Tijuana. I've seen him with my own eyes. It's really weird though — and I can't figure it out — but he's been hanging around a florist shop. He goes there regularly. He never leaves with any flowers, but he always has a smug smile on his face when he exits the shop. I've checked into it, and the shop isn't a front; it's a real shop that simply sells flowers."

Violet's lungs felt as if they had collapsed, pushing out all of their air. They refused to bring a breath back in, and Violet fought off the sensation of suffocating. Feeling her heart race and fear tingling in her fingertips and toes, she blurted out "Which one of you has been sending me the roses?"

Chapter 35

"What?" Shawn exclaimed as he motioned for the waiter to move past their table. No one was going to be ordering any food right now; they had too much to talk about.

"Violet, I'm confused," Santiago said. "Why would you think I was sending you roses? I didn't even know you were back in Tijuana."

"So, neither of you sent me the roses?" Violet was growing more concerned by the minute. "The notes were signed with just an 'S.' At first I really thought it was Sasqua... " Realizing what she was saying, her voice trailed off. The last thing she needed was to explain her overly friendly relationship with Everest. She had enough troubles dealing with the two men sitting at the table right now; she didn't need any more questions to be swimming in their eyes. "At first I thought it was a friend, but then I figured it was from one of you since it was signed with an S."

"You're saying that someone has been sending you roses with notes attached? And you never took action to know who they were from? What kind of notes are we talking about?" Shawn was alert. He glanced around the room before he pinned Violet with a serious stare. He was in full cop mode as he reprimanded her. "Violet! This is why I didn't want you coming here in the first place. You neglect your own safety and you downplay the warning signs of danger!"

"I'm not doing this again," Violet shook her head and put her hand up to stop him. Her eyebrows were drawn together and a scowl pulled down the corners of her mouth. "I will not have this conversation. Can we just stay focused?" Violet dismissed Shawn's reprimanding words and turned to Santiago. "Frank has been seen at a florist multiple times and I've been receiving roses. Is there a connection?"

"It's possible. Did you save the letters?"

Violet nodded yes, wondering why her cheeks were so hot. She'd kept the note cards simply because of the mystery of them, not because she wanted to treasure them or anything like that. And certainly not because she thought the police would want to see them in connection to their search for Frank.

Shawn extended his hand and wrapped his long fingers around Violet's forearm. "I'm sorry. I didn't mean to scold you. I just... " His eyes were luminous with emotion. "I just get scared by the thought that something could happen to you."

Violet placed her hand on top of his and squeezed. She smiled a sweet, small smile of understanding. "I'm fine,

Shawn. God's got great plans for us. He's watching out for me—and for you, too. At some point you've just got to trust in His plan. This has been a hard thing for me to learn and then to actually live out, but we really do need to trust."

Santiago cleared his throat. "I hate to break up whatever is going on between you two right now. But I have places I need to be; I need to wrap this up."

The jealousy that tinged his words seemed unfair. If he hadn't scared the living daylights out of her and actually tried to explain what had happened instead of demanding for her to kiss him as soon as Ricky had driven off, things may have been different between them. But he hadn't. He'd let her run away, he'd let her think such horrible things about him all this time. He'd let her try to forget him while she fell in love with another man. He had no right to be jealous.

The conversation shifted from the roses back to the details that Shawn was seeking. Violet couldn't quite tamp down her misgivings about the whole thing. Frank had fled to Mexico, and Shawn's sergeant told him to drop the case. But here she sat with two men who apparently held no desire to let Frank continue evading the law. They felt so certain that Frank needed to be stopped that neither of them cared about the security of their jobs; they were willing to take that risk.

As the conversation continued, Violet had the distinct feeling that the men knew more about Frank Smith and his past than they were telling her. The drive and passion that filled them as they discussed how to apprehend Frank filled her stomach with butterflies. Just what was Frank capable of? Was Rachel still in danger? *Am I in danger?*

"Wait, I'm confused," Violet interrupted the men who were so deep in conversation that they had forgotten she was there. "Why would Frank sign the notes with an S?"

Santiago looked at her for a moment before he answered with a matter of fact tone, "He goes by many different names, Violet; it doesn't matter how those notes were signed, we need to take all the precautions we can and treat this as if he's started threatening you, too."

Shawn nodded his head in agreement. "I'm going to need to see those letters, Violet."

"But the notes weren't threats. Why else would I think they could have come from you guys?" For some reason, Violet didn't want to give a voice to the memory of the one note that had reminded her of Frank. Maybe part of her was still in denial.

"Really, Violet? Sometimes you don't make sense." Shawn shook his head with incredulity. "The moment you saw Santiago, you panicked, yet you say the notes weren't threatening, and so they didn't make you think they were from Frank. But you thought they were maybe from Santiago? Until just a few minutes ago, Frank and Santiago were both dangerous men in your mind."

Violet clenched her fists; she was so frustrated she wanted to scream. Shawn was always making her feel stupid. Just because she wasn't a cop, it didn't mean he had the right to tell her she didn't understand things as well as he did. "There's a big difference! I don't love Frank!"

Violet's eyes grew round. She hadn't meant to say that. When would she ever learn to control herself? Would she forever be wishing she could take back words that were blurted out before really thinking them through?

For the second time since entering the restaurant, Violet covered her face with her hands in a gesture of vexation.

"I think I've gotten all the information I need." Shawn swallowed hard and stood up. He dug in his back pocket and pulled out his wallet. Placing some money on the table, he said, "The least we can do is pay for the use of their table." Turning on his heels he quickly headed for the door.

Violet sighed. When she stood up to follow him, her knees were weak and she longed to just sit back down and lay her head on the table and pretend her life wasn't so complicated. But she had to go after Shawn; she couldn't just let him walk out like that.

"Violeta," Santiago stood and reached for her. "I must talk with you."

Pain seared through Violet's chest. Her heart felt battered and bruised. How could she possibly choose between the two men? Speaking past the lump in her throat she tried to speak, but the single word sounded more like a sob, "No."

Without allowing herself the chance to change her mind, she ran out the door.

Chapter 36

"Shawn! Wait!" Violet called as she ran toward Shawn's retreating form. The strength that was portrayed in his every movement caused Violet's heart to quiver. The term *gentle giant* fit him, and she loved the way his strength was tempered with such a tender, noble heart. Had he wanted to, he could easily have picked a fight with Santiago and won. Between the two men, there was no doubt that Shawn was the stronger of the two, even though Santiago was a very muscular man.

Shawn stopped walking and turned toward Violet. Self-doubt shrouded his normally cheerful face. His hurt expression cut her to the core. She wanted to reassure him that he was the only one who held her heart, but how could she? She had to allow herself time to come to terms with the information that had been rapidly thrown at her today. Did a flame for Santiago still burn in her heart?

"We need to get you to your flight. Like I've said a million times, you're not safe here." There was no warmth in his voice, just a monotone, emotionless fact being spoken.

"Shawn, I... " Violet extended her hand to touch his arm. Deftly dodging her touch, he said, "Don't. Our relationship has been the most confusing thing I have ever experienced. I have no energy for it right now."

"And you think all this has been easy on me?"

"Honestly, Violet, I'm sure it hasn't. I can't imagine having such an indecisive heart." The sarcastic pity in his voice punched her and left her struggling to regain her emotional balance.

"I... but... that's not fair! You don't understand!"

"Violet, what *you* don't understand is that you are now the target of a very dangerous man. He's here in Tijuana and you need to leave."

"But, we were going to go get married. Are you just going to pretend we had never talked about that?"

Shawn tightly squeezed his eyes shut for a brief moment, causing his forehead to crinkle. After opening them he said, "I will only marry you if you tell me you feel nothing for Santiago... And I can see in your eyes that you are conflicted."

Violet could only stare at him. She searched his eyes as he searched hers, each hoping to see deep into the heart of the other. He deserved her complete devotion and she knew it. "You're right... It's probably for the best anyway. I think we would regret not having a church wedding." Her words were hollow, lacking any proof that she believed her own words. Deep down, she knew that she wouldn't regret an elopement nearly as much as she would regret losing this wonderful man. She knew she wanted to marry Shawn, but after learning the truth about Santiago, her confidence in that decision had been shaken.

She reached out for him again and this time he allowed her fingertips to trace the length of his arm before she reached up to touch his face. "Shawn, I really do love you. And I really do want to marry you... I just... the truth of who Santiago is kind of threw me for a loop."

Shawn leaned into her touch, letting her small hand cup his cheek. He moaned the tiniest bit before he spoke. "I love you, too. More than you know, Vi. Seeing all the different emotions march across your face back in that restaurant and then... when you practically said you love Santiago, I felt as if you had ripped my heart out. I don't want you to love him; I want you to love me! Oh, how I want you to love me! But I also want you to do so of your own decision. I need your love for me to be genuine."

Violet nodded, tears wetting the corners of her eyes. Shawn was a rare treasure and she knew it. She wanted to just tell him right then and there to forget about Santiago, but the words wouldn't come. "Can't we just get me a different flight? Can we go back to the beach and talk? I hate leaving things like this."

"Vi, I have to stay here and see if I can apprehend Frank." Violet started to interrupt him, but he put his hand up to stop her. "This whole thing is bigger than you understand and I will not listen to any argument you have about this." Violet watched as Shawn's face turned determined. "I will make sure there is justice. I will make sure he's stopped before anyone else gets hurt." His words were promises — promises that were uttered from his warrior's heart. He saw himself as a protector of the innocent and it was obvious that he had pursued a line of work that suited his personality best.

"You're right, this is bigger, and I don't understand. But stop evading my questions about Frank; you're not helping me by keeping information from me. Just tell me more about Frank and what he's doing! Please, help me understand."

Shawn drew in a deep breath. His jaw clenched and he shook his head. When he started to speak, he looked uncertain about sharing his information with her. "I have no concrete proof, but it appears that Frank is still obsessed with Rachel."

"But, the protective stalking order... hasn't that kept him away from her?"

Suddenly, Shawn looked at his watch. "Shoot!" He reached out and placed his hand on the small of Violet's back. "Let's go to my car. I need to get you to the airport. You better pray we get through the border quickly and get to the San Diego airport without any problems, or you're going to be late for your flight home."

Violet let him lead her to the car. She wanted to demand that she was staying here with him, that she refused to go home while he wandered the streets looking for Frank. But she knew she couldn't. Her practical side told her it was time to go home and make peace with Rachel. And she needed to apologize to her parents for leaving the country when they did not fully approve of the decision. While she was a grown woman, she still needed to honor her parents.

She also needed to allow Shawn to protect her. If he said she should go home, then she should. Every bad thing that had happened in Tijuana was the result of thinking she could do things on her own. It was time to allow other people to play important roles in her life. And right now, Shawn was playing the role of protector. He was sending her home to safety while he put a stop to the man who posed the threat.

When they had both buckled their seat belts and Shawn pulled away from the curb where he had parked, Violet turned and looked at him. "What makes you think Frank is still obsessed with Rachel? He hasn't broken the stalking order, has he?"

Shawn navigated the Tijuana streets with ease and Violet marveled at how he seemed to always know where he was going. Unlike her, he never seemed to be turned around or lost when driving in an unfamiliar city.

Shawn flexed his fingers on the steering wheel. "Violet, I'm not sure if I should tell you this. I really want to protect you from information that will cause you excessive worry or concern."

Irritation instantly filled her. "I'm not a fragile woman, Shawn. Haven't I proved that? Just tell me."

He hesitated, but finally acquiesced, "All right, but you must promise not to freak out or worry too much. Okay?"

"I promise."

"There has been a string of rapes and assaults in Southern California since Frank disappeared that night after he attacked Jacob." Even after all this time, just talking about that night still caused Shawn to wince.

"Okay. But there's more, isn't there? Stop beating around the bush and tell me for Pete's sake! There has to be more, because the last I heard, you all thought Frank had gone to Mexico. If he went to Mexico right after that night, then how is he responsible for this string of assaults?"

"That was just a guess based on a lead we had, and apparently he did have intentions of coming here since he is in Tijuana right now. But what I do know is that all the victims were pastor's daughters. And they all described their attacker as someone who fits Frank's physique perfectly. And..." Shawn's voice dropped. A battle was being waged; he was still uncertain he should continue.

A chill worked its way into Violet, leaving her cold and shivering. "And what?"

"Each victim said their attacker called them by the name of Rachel. Whoever is committing these crimes is a man who is obsessed with a woman named Rachel. The time frame, the physical description... all of it... it's too much to be a coincidence."

Chapter 37

Violet had promised Shawn that she would not worry. But it was a promise she had only been able to keep for about two minutes. Even now, an hour into her flight, Violet felt a big knot in the pit of her stomach.

She was looking out the window of the airplane, but the wispy white clouds did nothing to distract her mind from the heartbreaking news that women were being attacked. Just that knowledge alone was enough to greatly bother her, but when Shawn had told her the attacker was calling his victims Rachel, the knotted feeling in her stomach tightened. Hadn't Rachel been through enough already? How could a person become so obsessed that they would sink to this level?

Violet turned away from the window and rested her head on the back of her seat. She took a deep breath, pulling in extra air to completely fill her lungs. After holding it for a few seconds, she let her lungs slowly release until they were completely empty. If only a person could inhale hope and peace, while exhaling worry and fear. If Frank was still obsessed with Rachel, how many women would be hurt and assaulted in the wake of his cruel pursuit of her?

God, please stop this man from hurting anyone else. And please, protect Rachel. Give Shawn wisdom.

Violet's prayers were non-stop as she impatiently waited for her flight to end. While up in the air, she felt helpless. She wanted to do something to help insure that Rachel would be safe from Frank. And even though she knew Rachel's husband would be protecting her, Violet also knew that just like the first time around, there would be times when Rachel was alone even though everyone was working hard to keep her safe. And, she feared, it would be in those times when Frank would be the most likely to strike.

Shaking her head, Violet clenched her fist and tapped it on the armrest of her seat several times. It was so frustrating to think that the torment wasn't over. Shawn had been right. Memories of all the times she had argued with Shawn and accused him of being unnecessarily focused on catching Frank flashed through her mind. Guilt flooded her, making her heart squeeze in contrition.

Forgive me, God. Help me keep Rachel safe. Show me what to do. Show us all what to do.

* * ● ● ● ● * *

When Shawn had booked Violet's flight, he had also called Violet's parents to let them know when she would be arriving. Because she had planned to be in Tijuana indefinitely, Violet had taken a taxi to the airport when she had fled from her problems in the States. So it was a kind gesture for him to insure she would be greeted by a familiar face and spared the hassle of securing a taxi to finish her journey home.

A feeling of gratitude for Shawn's organization flitted through Violet's mind when she saw her mom walking toward her as she neared the baggage claim area. "Mom!" Violet held out her arms, feeling much like a small child returning home from summer camp. The lovely face of her mother had never looked so comforting.

"Oh, baby!" Cora said as she ran to embrace her daughter.

"I'm sorry, Mom. I'm really, really sorry." Violet choked out the apology as she began to cry. The whole time she had been in Tijuana, her damaged relationships had bothered her, but she didn't realize just how much until right now. "I should never have left the country with cross words between us."

"You're right, Violet." Cora spoke the truth in a loving way as she rubbed Violet's back. "But I forgive you and so does your dad."

Violet sighed in relief. It felt so good to be on her way to being free of that burden. She would have to re-build the trust between her parents and herself, but at least she had already taken the first step. With a faint smile, she left the soft, warm circle of her mother's arms, wiped the tears from her face and turned to watch the luggage creep past on the conveyor belt. Piece after piece, the luggage went by, but she hadn't seen her suitcase yet. She felt concerned; surely the airline hadn't lost her luggage again!

But thankfully, just a few minutes later, the familiar suitcase could be seen. Taking a few steps toward the conveyor belt, Violet reached out and scooped up her suitcase. "All right, Mom, let's go!"

As the two women made their way to Cora's car, they made small talk and Cora commented on how tan Violet had become. Violet laughed and made a joke about the fog that encased the coastal town they lived in. While they did have sunny days on the northern coast of California, most days included fog and wind. Almost as steady as clockwork, there was usually fog in the morning, wind in the afternoon, and more fog as the last light of the sun dispersed in the evening.

The hum of tires on blacktop made the silence between mother and daughter even more profound. Cora never was a very talkative person. She was the quiet one who sat back and watched those around her. And Violet loved her mom for that quality, because it caused her to be perceptive and incredibly caring. But today, Violet didn't like the silence. She wished her mom would start talking, or turn on the radio, anything to stop the words that wanted to spring from her mouth.

Violet began to hum. Maybe if she hummed she could get her mind onto something else. But it didn't work. Her absent minded song tapered off and soon Violet began nervously shifting in her seat.

"For goodness sakes, girlie, just say whatever it is that's bothering you," Cora laughed.

Violet pursed her lips and glanced sideways at her mom before turning her gaze to her hands that were lying in her lap. How could she say what she was thinking? The words had never been allowed to go farther than her own mind, even though she had wanted to say them for over a year.

"Mom, I know it hasn't been easy for you and Dad, but I want you to know that what Vivian did had nothing to do with you guys. I think she ran away because of me."

Shock caused Cora to gasp. "Why would you ever say such a thing?"

"Mom, come on. You saw it. My whole life's goal was to be better than Vivian. At every milestone and important event, there I was, rubbing it in her face that I was better. And then, when she ran away with that boy, I walled up my heart and swore I would never stoop so low. But it was a farce, mom. I knew the things that ran through my mind. I wanted to be with boys just as much as she did."

Cora grasped the steering wheel tight enough to turn her knuckles white. She had straightened her back and sat at full attention while she drove. It was apparent that she wanted to reach out and take Violet in her arms.

"Sweetheart. Oh, my dear child. You are not responsible for your sister. Yes, you were very competitive. And you naturally excelled at things she didn't, and so that made it hard for her. But you cannot blame yourself for Vivian running away. That was her own choice, sweetie."

Violet still looked at her hands, focusing on a damaged fingernail. After picking at the broken nail for a bit, she clenched and released her hands a few times in nervous frustration. "Yeah, but my choices were awful. I've spent so much time competing with her, simply because I could. I took joy in the fact that I was better than her, I was so self-righteous. But Mom, I should never have been doing that. Mom, what happened in Tijuana last time showed me how flawed my thinking was."

"What do you mean?" Cora perked up at the mention of the past. Violet knew her mom had desperately wanted to know what had happened.

"I fell in love, Mom. And everything just crumbled before my eyes. And I realized that I was no better than Vivian."

"Sweetheart, how does falling in love make you... oh, I see." Disappointment tinged Cora's words. Violet had been taught from a young age about how God viewed relationships between men and women. And Violet knew her parent's desire was for their daughters to follow God's instructions and remain abstinent before marriage because failing to wait for that intimacy could bring heartache and pain. And those results were displayed in Vivian's life.

Violet began to laugh in relief. She had made some foolish choices, but at least she had been spared from that heartache. "No, Mom, you don't see. I didn't mean what you are thinking. I meant that I fell in love with the man who kidnapped me. Or so I thought."

"What?" Cora's eyes were round and in her surprise she accidently stomped down on the accelerator pedal as she turned to look at her daughter. Quickly turning her eyes back to the road and adjusting her speed she said, "None of this makes sense. You've got better judgment than that. Tell me what happened."

The rest of the drive home was spent with Violet sharing each and every little detail of what had happened both times she was in Tijuana. And as she shared, her burden lifted. The guilt and shame she had felt for so long melted away in the light of truth. She had not fallen in love with an evil man. And she didn't need to worry about being better than Vivian. She simply needed to strive to do the best she could at living out God's plan for her own life.

God, thank you for teaching me. And for being patient with me as I took so long to learn such simple truths.

"Mom, I need to find Vivian. I need to tell her I'm sorry."

Chapter 38

Staying true to her nature, Rachel pulled Violet into her arms and freely offered forgiveness the moment she opened her front door to find Violet standing there with a repentant look on her face.

After Violet's tearful, heartfelt, and humble apology, she was ushered into the house and encouraged to take a seat on the couch while Rachel fixed them both a cup of tea. As Violet listened to the bumping and clunking coming from the kitchen, she looked around and admired the homey atmosphere that Rachel had brought to the house. What was previously a typical bachelor's house was now an immaculately clean, yet very inviting home that smelled of laundry soap and delicious treats baking in the oven.

Violet soon got tired of waiting all alone and stood to make her way into the kitchen. "Is that a nutmeg cake I smell?" Violet's mouth watered just thinking about the moist, decadent vanilla cake that was fragrant with nutmeg.

"It sure is. Hubby just loves those cakes and I can't help but spoil the man!" Rachel was glowing as she laughed, "I'm sorry, I'm just being a mushy newlywed!"

"What does a girl have to do to get a piece of that cake?" Violet asked as she walked into the kitchen.

Smiling an indulgent smile, Rachel quickly moved to serve up two large pieces of the coveted dessert. She motioned for Violet to grab the tea tray. "Let's go eat and drink in comfort! I'm so glad you're back... and I'm glad that we are on speaking terms again... I've missed you so!"

They both settled into a comfortable spot in the living room and took a few moments to savor a couple bites of the cake. Violet felt a small stab of jealousy as she looked at her beautiful, confident friend. Rachel had an air about her, she had this way of being radiant and calm no matter what life brought. And while Violet prided herself in her practicality—which Rachel sometimes lacked—she was aware that practicality doesn't make a person's countenance glow with God's love like Rachel's did.

Ever since she had known Rachel, Violet could see that it was her yielded heart that set her apart. But Violet had always been afraid to let go of the control she had over her own heart; even though she knew that being yielded to God was what made Rachel the kind of person that Violet admired.

Realizing how quickly she'd slipped back into comparing herself and competing with those around her, Violet laughed a sad, self-conscious laugh. She had a long road ahead of her. But at least she was finally choosing to see life differently. And one of the first steps was to share her weakness so her closest friend could hold her accountable.

"You know Rach, I've always been a bit jealous of you."

"What?" Rachel was incredulous.

"Your ability to be filled with joy during your battle with Frank has always been a mystery to me. And for a long time I've wished that I could be like you. You are always so confident in God and the work He is doing in your life. You never seem to be shaken by what others think of you."

When Rachel just shrugged off the compliments, Violet went on to share the lessons God had taught her about comparing herself to others. She told Rachel what had happened when she was kidnapped and how her desire to be better than Vivian had fueled her shame and secrecy. She knew Misty's life could be potentially jeopardized if the wrong people found out what had really happened, but Violet had used that as a good excuse to hide her shame and guilt.

"Oh, Violet," Rachel said with sympathy. "You shouldn't be embarrassed or feel guilty by the fact that you fell in love, even if it was to a bad man. Everyone makes mistakes from time to time. And it's not like you stayed in the relationship after you learned the truth." Rachel took a sip of her tea. Setting down the cup, she continued encouraging Violet, "It's what a person does with the mistakes they make that counts, and you made the right choice by ending your relationship with Santiago as soon as you found out who he really was."

Violet looked at Rachel and smiled. It felt good to hear that Rachel didn't think less of her now that she knew the story. "But, you haven't heard it all."

"There's more?" Rachel looked surprised. "Just how many secrets have you been keeping?"

A mischievous smile crept across Violet's face. "Oh, just about a hundred more."

"Oh, brother!"

"Seriously though, I've told you all my secrets. What I have to tell you now just happened yesterday. But it's still bothering me... " Violet looked into Rachel's hazel eyes, hoping she would find some profound wisdom to answer all her questions. "I really don't know what to do. I saw Santiago yesterday—the first time since I ran away from him that scary day—and after I stopped panicking, he told me that he's a police detective. Rachel, he didn't kidnap me, he saved my life!"

Rachel looked as if she was uncertain of what to think about this newest piece of information. "Um, didn't you just tell me he was super charming and persuasive? Maybe he's still lying to you. After all, do police detectives have the freedom to do the things he's claimed? Do they really go around 'buying' women's freedom?"

Violet nodded her head in disagreement. "I know he wasn't lying because he was Shawn's contact." Violet went on to share how they had gone to the restaurant to meet up with one of Shawn's friends, only to discover it was Santiago they were meeting with.

"Wow. Talk about awkward! What did Shawn think about Santiago being your ex-boyfriend? I bet Shawn was so jealous, even though he knows you only love him!"

Violet refused to look Rachel in the eye. And for a moment she considered just ignoring the comment. But, she knew her friend would simply sit there and wait for a reply. "Shawn didn't actually take the news very well. I didn't help much either when I basically said I still love Santiago."

Rachel sucked in a gasp. "You what?"

"It just kind of slipped out and once I said it, there was no going back."

"But, do you really love Santiago? How can you love two men at the same time? Did you stop loving Shawn?" Rachel was full of questions and they tumbled out one right after the other.

Giant tears rolled down Violet's face. She bit her lip while looking at the ceiling. *Do I even know what I feel anymore?*

"I love Shawn, I know that. But, I think I still might love Santiago, too. I know it sounds strange, but I love them each for different reasons."

"What are you going to do?" Rachel whispered. The tone of her voice held no reproach or condemnation.

"I don't really know. Santiago was my first love, and there's some special bond there. But, after thinking he was evil all this time, I wonder if I would truly be able to trust him."

"But, was it really his fault?"

"No," the word came out as a sigh. "I guess I just need to pray about it and see what God tells me. The last thing I want is to step out of God's plan for my life."

"There are a lot of things you should consider, you know that... but which man supports your desire for missions the most? Is one man more devoted to God than the other?"

"Well, that's just it. I'm not even sure where God is calling me right now. I'm not certain, but I almost feel like my time of service in Tijuana needs to come to an end. I think I need to spend some time working on my personal relationship with God before I jump right back into missions. The past couple of weeks have shown me a great deal, and I see now that I have a lot of maturing to do. I haven't handled things very well, and I certainly need to learn how to be transparent in my relationships—all of them—not just my human ones, but my relationship with God, too."

Rachel looked at Violet with tenderness. "I think just admitting you need to grow is a sign of the growth you've made already. Just a month ago you would have sat here and told me you had life all figured out."

Violet couldn't deny Rachel's statement. It had taken a lot for her to come to the point where she could openly admit she had aspects of her life that had never been fully surrendered to God.

Slowly, the conversation drifted from the topic of ministry opportunities for Violet and her need to mature, to Rachel's work at her father's church there in Casper, California. Although Rachel's husband worked in the larger city of Fort Bragg, they had purchased a home in Casper so Rachel could be close to her job and her parents.

"Rachel, has Shawn told you anything about Frank?" Violet rapidly changed the subject, suddenly feeling a strong need to know what Rachel's thoughts about Frank were.

"Yes, Violet. He's told me everything he feels I should know about the case. It breaks my heart to know that it's probably Frank out there ruining the lives of other women. He should have been stopped here."

A solemn mood settled over the young women as their minds took them to dark places, imagining the things the poor women had suffered.

When Rachel spoke again, her voice waivered with the strong emotions she tried to hold back. "I'm taking care to make sure that I am safe. But really, I'm not very worried for myself; it's everyone else. More innocent people are being hurt, Violet! Due to the victims being called Rachel regardless of their real names, it's obvious that he's still stuck on me. But he also is showing that he is afraid of the protective order since he hasn't bothered me... since... " Rachel dropped her gaze and looked to the floor. It was obvious that it was still hard for her to talk about that terrifying night.

"Don't you worry he might just show up here one day?"

"He might," Rachel shrugged.

Uncertain how her friend would respond, Violet knew she had to tell her about the roses. Rachel had to know that Frank was creeping closer to home than she knew. Rachel needed to be prepared for that day he would return. In

Violet's mind, there was no *if* about it; her gut told her their struggle with Frank was anything but over.

"Rachel, when I was in Tijuana, someone was sending me roses. Santiago and Shawn think they may have been from Frank and… they're worried I'm on his list of victims.

Rachel sagged in her chair, looking much like a balloon after all of its air is let out.

"First Jacob and now, you," She whispered. "He's going to hurt the people I love, just to punish me for not loving him."

Chapter 39

Rachel's words echoed in Violet's mind as she drove home. Parking her car in her parents' driveway, Violet tried to stuff back the unsettled feelings that Rachel's words had stirred up. Was that really what Frank was doing? Was he sending Rachel a message through the attacks and assaults of other women? It was a concept she had overlooked. She had thought Frank had gone crazy and was thinking the other women were Rachel. But what if he wasn't crazed and confused? Maybe he was cold and calculated. *Is each rape and each attack a threat, a foretelling of what Rachel should expect?*

Removing her keys from the ignition, she stepped out of the car and walked to the house. Since neither of her parents would be home until later in the day, she unlocked the door and walked into the empty house.

The silence was creepy. After talking about Frank and then thinking about him on the drive home, Violet's senses were on full alert. Each creak of the house or rumble from the refrigerator caused her heart to jump and her pulse to race.

This is how Rachel felt every day for almost two years... skittish and bothered by every little noise.

Asking God to help her stop feeling spooked, she walked down the hall to her bedroom. There had been times when she chafed at the fact that she still lived with her parents. But between her missions trips, online college classes, and the drama of Frank, she and her parents had agreed that it was in her best interest to stay with them. And once she had started dating Shawn, she had figured it would only be a matter of time until she would be married and moving to a house of her own. No need to spend money on renting an apartment; it was much wiser to save up the money for after she was married.

Violet sat down on her bed and sighed. Until she figured out what was in her heart, there wasn't going to be a wedding anytime soon. She had made a lot of progress in her spiritual life lately, but she still had no answers when it came to the romantic part of her life.

Shawn was a wonderful person for so many reasons, but ever since Frank attacked Jacob and then went missing, Shawn was filled with anger. And that anger bothered her. If he failed to address it, it would eventually consume him — and whoever he married.

But was Santiago any better? While he seemed to have more self-control when it came to anger, there was still so much mystery surrounding him. With all the excitement of seeing him just yesterday, she realized she still hadn't been told Santiago's last name. And how could he be a police detective and be rescuing girls from sex trafficking at the same time? There were so many things that just didn't quite fit into place for her.

Violet lay back on her bed and stared at the ceiling for a while, her thoughts springing back and forth between the two men. She had known Shawn for a longer period of time. But Santiago was so very charming. Shawn's life wasn't a mystery; he was very much a "you-get-what-you-see" type of person. Santiago, however, seemed less likely to become angry. It would appear his tendency was toward melancholy. She clearly remembered the day on the beach when he had stared into the water and asked her if she ever felt like helping people was a waste of time, as if what she could offer would never be enough to make a real change. Now that she knew the truth surrounding his vocation, she could see that he had been heartbroken that day. The number of women who needed rescuing was great and he was feeling helpless to free them all.

She could think things through all she liked, but the only thing that would really shed unbiased light on the situation would be prayer. She rolled to her side and then slipped off the edge of the bed onto her knees. Feeling at a loss for how to even start praying, she knelt in silence, fully aware of how scattered she was. Soon, however, she began to pour out her thoughts to the One who already knew them. She admitted her brokenness and her need to be changed. She begged God to empty her out and to fill her up with His spirit. She wanted to have that yielded heart that she so admired in Rachel.

Before she even knew it, she had spent over an hour in prayer. She would have continued resting in the presence of God, but the sound of a car outside the house pulled her mind from her prayers. Amazed at how quickly time had passed while she was in prayer, she stood up and went to see who was outside.

Just as she was nearing the front door, the bell rang. Even though she knew someone was coming up to the door, the noise still startled her, causing her to jump. Placing a hand over her racing heart, she giggled a little at how silly she must have looked.

But when she opened the door, her giggles were silenced and her smile vanished.

Standing on her doorstep was the local florist. A single red rose was held in his hand.

Violet barely had enough self-control to wait for the florist to hand her the rose. She almost reached out to snatch up the card that was attached to the vase to read it right there in front of him. But she forced herself to smile as she waited for him to place the vase in her hand.

"Someone's glad to see that you're home, Violet." The man smiled and winked. He was unaware that the sender was most likely a criminal.

The small town dynamics of just about everyone knowing who you are irritated Violet at the moment. It would seem that the whole town was aware of her coming and going. But what should she expect when half of its citizens attended the same church she did?

"Thanks, Mr. Carter." Violet forced herself to be polite. "Have a good day."

As soon as she closed the door behind Mr. Carter, Violet set the rose on the tile floor of the home's entryway and ripped open the tiny envelope. When she saw the haphazardly written words, Violet's stomach turned. She gulped a few times to stave off the feeling of nausea.

After reading all the unwanted letters Rachel had gotten from Frank, Violet knew she would recognize Frank's penmanship for the rest of her life. The way he mixed lower and upper case letters all throughout his words and sentences, along with his atrocious spelling, made for a very unique way of writing. And it was unmistakable that this note was written by him.

Among several ink smears, and what looked like a sticky set of fingerprints made up of peanut butter and jelly, was a hastily written message.

"WeLComb hOme VioLEt. BothE RAchEl anD
Me ArE Hapy YoU Are BakK in CasPeR."

At first, all she could think about was the fact that the florist in Tijuana must have been writing the notes for him. All the other roses came with very neatly penned messages. Had they looked like this one, she would have called Shawn as soon as the first one had been delivered.

Suddenly, Violet's mind started to race. If she could prove this was from Frank, then the fact that he mentioned Rachel would prove that he was in violation of the protective order Rachel had in place.

Throwing the letter to the floor, Violet ran to her room. Frantically searching through her purse, she finally found the small scrap of paper that held Shawn's hotel name and phone number. He had asked her to call him if she heard any information she thought he could use, and this was certainly something he should know about.

Clutching the paper in her hand, she walked back down the hall to the phone and pressed in the long, international number as fast as she could. Her hands began to shake as she waited for him to answer. One ring turned into two and then three. What if he wasn't there?

On the tenth ring he picked up. "Hello?" His voice sounded gravelly with sleep.

"Shawn, it's Violet."

"Hey, babe. I was just thinking about you."

Violet could hear the smile in his voice and her heart warmed a little. "Hey, I got another rose."

All Violet could hear was a bunch of muffled scratching and muttering. Then there was a thunk and the sound of bed springs squeaking.

"Sorry Vi, I dropped the phone. Are you telling me Frank sent you another rose?"

"Yes, and this time it's his penmanship and he mentioned Rachel."

"Yes! Violet! This is just what I need!" His excitement was contagious and Violet's hopes began to rise. Maybe things had gone well in Tijuana. Maybe Shawn had obtained what he was looking for. Was it possible that everything would be over soon?

"Vi, baby," Shawn suddenly turned stoic. "Promise me you will call the police after we hang up. You've got to report this and all the other roses and notes. Look, I'm coming home tomorrow, but I need to know you won't be alone tonight. I think Frank followed you back into the States. He very well could be watching your house right now."

As Shawn expressed his concern that Frank was watching her, she felt her optimism plummet to the ground like a poorly folded paper airplane. Suddenly, her home didn't feel comforting any more. The windows seemed like traitors and the doors appeared inadequate at keeping her safe.

As the cold prickle of fear crawled up her spine, she thanked God for men like Shawn and the other dedicated police officers who worked hard to defend the innocent.

Chapter 40

The night had been a long one for Violet. Even though her parents had been sleeping in their room just down the hall from hers, Violet had still been on edge and was only able to doze off occasionally throughout the night. There was too much to think about, too much to worry about.

The message that came with the rose had been disturbing and it only added to the unsettled feelings that had been plaguing her ever since she had seen Santiago.

Swinging her legs off the side of the bed, Violet yawned as she sat up. Brilliant sunshine was streaming through the cracks in her curtains, telling her that it was time to get out of bed. She would need a lot of coffee to get enough energy to face what the day would hold. Shawn was coming home in just a few hours and then they were going to go to the police station together to turn in the evidence they had. Violet would bring the cards that had come with the roses, and Shawn was bringing the information he had gathered in Mexico.

Not even caring to look in the mirror, Violet went straight to the kitchen for a cup of coffee. Her mind was so groggy, even the mundane task of getting dressed seemed like too much work right now.

When Violet stepped into the kitchen, she was greeted by her father.

"Good morning, sunshine! How's my girl today?" Greg Thompson's bright and cheerful attitude was in deep contrast to hers.

"Morning, Dad; I think I'm more asleep than awake right now," she mumbled as she walked over to him to give him a hug. As her arms wrapped around his neck, she nuzzled his freshly shaved cheek that smelled of soap and aftershave. No matter how old she got, when she was being hugged by her dad she felt just like a six year old little girl. "I love you, Dad." She whispered before leaving his embrace. Hugs were wonderful, but at the moment, coffee was more important.

As she poured herself a cup of the fragrant, dark brew, Violet thought about the conversation she'd had with her parents the night before. First she'd told them of the rose that Mr. Carter had delivered and her talk with Shawn, followed by her quick call into the police. Then she'd taken the time to talk in depth with her parents about all the things that had happened between her first trip to Tijuana and the one she had just returned from. It had been a long conversation, but a needed one. Her parents had so many questions, and for the first time in over a year, Violet had finally felt free to answer them all.

"Dad, do you think God is disappointed in me?" Violet asked reflectively, her voice barely loud enough for him to hear.

"Are you still thinking about our conversation last night?"

Violet nodded and took a sip from her cup.

Greg looked at his daughter a long time, searching for just the right words. "I'm not certain 'disappointed' is quite the right word. I believe with my whole heart that God wants us to strive to be people who bring Him glory. And I believe that He wants us to work hard at being the person He wants us to be. But I think that when God looks at His children, I think He sees a whole lot more than just the moment we are in. He sees what's in our hearts and He knows where we will eventually end up. And while it's vital that we make sure we keep very short accounts with God, striving to be honest about our sins and failures, I think God sees His kids through 'grace-colored' glasses because the blood of Jesus changes everything."

Violet couldn't help but smile at her Dad's answer. Since he was an accountant, he always liked to use that analogy whenever he talked about asking God for forgiveness. But his grace comment was new to her. "I like that... 'grace-colored' glasses. Boy, am I grateful for God's grace... "

Suddenly there was a knock at the door. Both Violet and her dad looked at the clock hanging on the wall above the little table in the kitchen. Even though the house had a formal dining room, the worn table in the kitchen was where the family took most of their meals and enjoyed their morning coffee.

"Who would be visiting at this time of the morning?" Violet asked her dad as he rose to answer the door.

"I'm not sure." Greg's long legs brought him to the door quickly. He discreetly looked through the window at the side of the door and turned back to Violet with a huge grin splitting his face. "It's your favorite man. Shawn's here already!"

Violet shrieked and stood up. "He can't see me like this! Dad, don't open that door! Wait until I'm in my room."

Greg laughed and teased Violet by making a show of unlocking the door.

Violet ran down the hall laughing. But there was also a part of her that wondered if something was wrong. Shawn wasn't supposed to be back in Casper for another couple of hours.

· ◦ ◦ ◉ ◦ · ·

Violet could hear Shawn making small talk with her father. She had quickly changed from her pajamas into a pair of jeans and a dressy, light-weight sweater. She walked quickly from her room to the bathroom where she brushed her teeth and pulled her long, blonde hair back into a French braid. Looking in the mirror, she could see that her cheeks were rosy.

Why am I blushing like a love-sick teenager?

Once she was satisfied with her reflection in the mirror, she stepped out into the hall and made her way to the living room where the men were visiting.

The moment Shawn saw her he stood up. He reached out his right hand and walked toward her. "Hey, Babe!"

When she was near enough, he pulled her into his arms. Although he tried to hide it, Violet knew he was leaning in to smell her hair as she tucked her head under his chin. The sweet gesture of love and adoration made her wonder what was in his heart. Was he as confused as she was? Why did he feel he had to be discreet about enjoying her fragrance?

"You came back early," she said matter of fact.

"I did. Vi, I really need to talk to you." Shawn glanced around the room, looking at Greg and then cleared his throat. "I want to talk about… us."

"Okay."

"Have you eaten?" Shawn asked eagerly. Violet assumed he was hoping to take her some place private so they could talk without her parents listening in.

"No, I haven't eaten. Did you want to go out for a bite?"

Shawn smiled at her as he nodded. Gratitude was in his eyes.

"Just let me go get my shoes on and then I'll be ready," Violet said as she made her way back to her room.

Moments later, they bid goodbye to Greg and walked out to Shawn's car. Violet felt as if she had a hundred butterflies in her stomach; Shawn was going to ask her for answers. Did she love him, or did she still love Santiago?

Chapter 41

The muffled chatter and random sounds contained in the little mom and pop diner gave Shawn and Violet a sense of privacy. Everyone around them seemed too interested in each other, or the food on their tables, to eavesdrop on a conversation between two lovers.

"Vi, I came back early because I just really need to get things out in the open." Shawn was serious, causing Violet to nervously fidget with the napkin in her lap.

"Okay. Then let's do that." She had no idea what he wanted to talk about, but she knew if they were going to move forward in their relationship, then it was imperative that this conversation take place, whatever it was.

Shawn reached out across the table, the back of his hand resting on the scuffed table top. He wiggled his fingers, beckoning Violet to place her hand in his.

Swallowing back a jumbled mess of emotions, she reached out and entwined her fingers within his.

"You've known me for a while now, but you never really knew me before Frank was following Rachel." When Violet nodded in agreement, he continued, "It's just that... well, I... Vi, I'm not an angry man. At least I wasn't before."

Shawn's words shocked her and she brought her gaze up from their hands and stared into his eyes. "You have your moments, but you're not an overly angry man."

"But I am. I let my anger over Frank slowly grow and simmer, and then... " Shawn let out a sigh. "Then he attacked Jacob, and it was so, so *gruesome*. There was so much blood. Blood, everywhere. All over the car and the road."

Violet's eyes filled with tears as she watched the dear man in front of her struggle for composure. She began rubbing her fingers back and forth against his in a loving way. "I know honey, I'm sorry. It must have been terrible to see your friend like that."

Staring at a spot on the back of the booth just to the right of Violet's head, Shawn seemed lost in his thoughts. Finally he spoke, "I've never told you why I became a cop."

Several minutes passed. Violet continued to gently rub his fingers while Shawn continued to stare and remember.

"I was just a kid, I was only twelve. I remember the day as if it were just yesterday. I was riding my bike home from school one day; I can still feel the warm sun on my face and smell the fumes of cars as they drove past. I turned the corner from the sidewalk of a busy street onto an alley that served as a short-cut to my house. I only got about a quarter of the way through that alley when I saw him."

Shawn's voice quavered and his lips twisted. "There, lying in a huge pool of blood, was my best friend's father."

"What happened?" Violet forced the question through her stiff lips, lips that wanted to only frown.

"It was a gang-related act of violence that left a widow and a young boy to grieve a loss they should have never endured." Bitterness colored Shawn's words, making them biting and cold. "My friend was never the same after that… and neither was I."

"Oh, Shawn, honey, I'm so very sorry." Violet felt helpless. She had no idea what to say.

"When I saw Jacob lying in the road, all my childish rage and anger over the injustice of that senseless, despicable act rushed to the surface. Vi, I don't know how to control it. I've stuffed it back for so many years, and now it's running wild in my life. I've begged God to forgive me. And now, I'm begging you. Please, forgive me for being such a bully. For being rude and angry and bossing you around."

Violet wrapped her hands around his shaking hand that still rested on the table and squeezed it before drawing it to her lips. Tenderly kissing his calloused, masculine fingers, she smiled a watery smile. "Thank you. For letting me see into your heart. For being humble enough to ask for forgiveness."

Violet wanted to continue speaking, but the waitress brought their food, interrupting their intimate moment.

As the plates clunked onto the table, Violet and Shawn thanked the waitress. After offering a prayer of gratitude to

God for the food set before them, they each began to feast on the pancakes, eggs, and bacon they had ordered.

"I'm going to apologize to my Sarge; I need to get him on board with this investigation rather than just go out there and do whatever I want. I'm done letting my anger fuel my actions. I need his help."

Violet's heart thrilled to hear this news. She had worried over Shawn's decision to place his job in jeopardy. If he were to get discharged, how could he help anyone? "I'm glad. Getting help is always a good idea." As the truth of her words hung in the air, she marveled at how deeply she felt them. If nothing else, her time in Tijuana had taught her that even the smartest and strongest people benefitted from gathering information and accepting help from others.

Shawn went on to tell Violet some more details of what he'd done after she had flown out of Tijuana, explaining how he had gone to the florist and asked for her to identify the sender of the roses from a group of photos. Without hesitation, Frank's picture was the one she had pointed to.

The familiar twist of fear caused Violet's appetite to vanish. "So I've been Frank's target this whole time."

Shawn simply pursed his lips and dipped his head in reply. He didn't need to say anything; Violet could see he agreed with her statement.

Shawn took a heaping bite of eggs and slowly chewed. He motioned for Violet to eat as well, but she feared taking another bite would only make her nervous stomach feel worse.

After wiping his face with a napkin, Shawn sat back in his seat and leveled his gaze on Violet. "So have you decided?"

The question confused Violet for the briefest moment. But the vulnerable look on Shawn's face told her what he was asking about. "Shawn, I love you. But... I... I need just a little more time to pray."

"Santiago is coming to Casper today; he's going with me to talk to the Sarg. today." The monotone of his voice betrayed the feelings about Santiago that he was trying to hide. He leaned in to get closer to Violet. "I need to know whether I should be rejoicing over the fact that you love me, or mourning over the loss of the greatest love of my life."

The raw emotion moved Violet. She wanted to tell him that he was the greatest love of her life and that he needn't worry. *But can I honestly say that?*

"Vi, I'm trying to be victorious over this anger in my life. But I would be lying if I were to claim that I will let Santiago have you without him knowing my opinion on the matter."

The declaration slammed into Violet's chest with a force that took her breath away. The investigation of Frank depended on these two men working together in cooperation. If she handled things poorly, the result would be far reaching.

Chapter 42

The meeting with the sergeant had obviously gone well. While Violet had not been included in the conversation between the three men, she had seen both Shawn and Santiago smiling as they left the man's office, a sure sign that things had gone in their favor.

I just hope I can find a way to keep both those men smiling and willing to work together peaceably in spite of the fact that I will choose one over the other.

While the men had been in their meeting, Violet had been answering a myriad of questions concerning the roses she had received. She sat in a rickety chair across from a young officer; the desk between them was scattered with papers, a silent testimony to the man's tendency toward clutter. Violet was relieved that the cards she had turned in as evidence were safely placed in a file waiting to be seen by the sergeant.

Violet was grateful that the officer felt her information was important, but she had grown weary of his repeated questions. And when she saw that Santiago and Shawn were finished with their meeting, she was even more eager to be finished with hers as well.

As Shawn walked up to the desk where she sat, he looked at Violet and then the officer she was working with. "Are you almost finished? I need to run across town and pick something up. It's important that I do it soon."

The young man looked up from the paperwork he had been filling out. "We still have a few more questions to go over."

Violet looked at Shawn, trying to keep her impatience from showing. "Go on ahead. If you're not back by the time I'm done, I'll just sit out front and enjoy the sunshine while I wait for you to come get me."

Quickly glancing at Santiago, who was standing across the room, Shawn shrugged his shoulders. He bent down to kiss Violet on the top of the head. "Ok, I'll try to hurry."

Violet's eyes trailed Shawn as he walked out of the police station. She wondered for a bit about where he was going, but when she was asked another question she forced herself to turn away from Shawn's retreating form. As she turned, her eye caught a glimpse of Santiago. He smiled and waved and then walked out the same door Shawn had used.

These men, they're going to give me gray hair before it's all said and done!

"Miss Thompson," the officer said impatiently, "We really need to stay focused here."

"Yes, I'm sorry." Violet sighed. "What was the question?"

276

• ◦ ◉●◉ ◦ •

Violet had finally been released from the interview. Breathing a sigh of relief, she was happy to know that everything had been documented. Surely with all the information, along with the sergeant's permission for Shawn to pursue the case, Frank would be apprehended soon. Hopefully the end of the string of assaults was close at hand. Maybe soon they could all breathe a little easier instead of bracing themselves for what might happen next.

Violet walked out the door, and looked around to see where she wanted to sit while she waited for Shawn to return. The grounds around the police station weren't exactly well maintained, but there were some pretty flowers blooming here and there, as well as a few benches to choose from.

"Violeta."

The sound of Santiago's voice coming from behind her startled Violet, causing her to gasp as she spun on her heels to look at him. "Santiago! You scared me."

The handsome man smiled a lazy smile. "I guess I've made a habit of that."

"That's not funny," Violet scolded while remembering all the times she had been filled with paralyzing fear because of him.

Remorse quickly replaced his playful attitude as Santiago took a deep bow. "My sincerest apologies, my lady."

The swoop and flourish of the bow took Violet's mind back to the first time she had met Santiago. Warmth spread through her as she thought about the love that had bloomed between them. But that love had been crushed just like a flower under a careless foot. Santiago's lack of communication had caused Violet's heart to turn from him. But now, standing in front of him, she knew without a doubt that the tender blossom of love could be coaxed back to life — if she were to allow him to make amends.

"Violeta, can we talk?" His dark eyes were pleading.

Violet nodded yes and let him guide her to the stone bench under a large oak tree. He waited until she sat down before he settled himself next to her. "I know that time and misinformation has damaged what we once enjoyed. But, I stayed here today because I want to remedy that. I sit here next to you, ready and willing to answer any questions you may have."

"Ok, what is your last name?"

Santiago arched his eyebrows in a gesture that told Violet he thought it was an easy question. "That's a fair enough question. It's Fox."

"Wow. And here I thought you were really going to talk to me." Violet's braid swayed from side to side as she shook her head in disgust. She stood up and started to walk away.

I should have known getting information from him was a waste of time. I can't believe he thinks I'm that gullible.

After just a few steps, she turned back, unable to let him get by with such a flippant answer. All her past hurts bubbled up and spilled over, taking on the form of anger. "Do you really think I'm going to believe that? After all you put me through? Look at you! You're not Anglo for

Pete's sake! Couldn't you have come up with a better lie than that?" She began to walk away again, satisfied that he knew just how angry she felt.

"Violeta." Santiago's voice held patience, but it was still tinged with a touch of condescension. "Has it never occurred to you that maybe I am. Do you know my father's heritage?"

Violet stopped walking and stood with her back toward him, uncertain whether she should hear him out or just forget it all and leave him standing there.

"I know it seems odd, but it's true. My father is Anglo and my last name truly is Fox." Santiago stood up and came near Violet. She could feel the warmth from his body, he stood so close. "Please, you need to give me a chance, hear me out. I'm not lying to you; I never have."

He leaned in with his last words and she could feel his breath on the back of her neck. Part of her longed for him to reach out and bury her in his arms, but the other part knew it would be unwise.

Taking a few steps to distance herself from him, she spun around to look him in the eye. "If you are a police detective then why were you rescuing prostitutes? Isn't that getting your job descriptions confused?"

Relief flooded Santiago's face. "This is your concern? That my job description doesn't match what I actually do?"

Impatience marched through Violet's mind. "Yes. It is!"

"Ok... all right. I did give you the simple description of my past when we were in the restaurant. Time didn't allow for me to go into full detail, but now I can. And I want to.

I want nothing to be left unspoken between us." Santiago flashed her one of his most charming smiles. "I was serving as a police detective, working in connection with the San Diego police department. That was three years ago. But I got sickened by watching woman after woman be abused, murdered... you name it... at the hands of cruel, heartless men." His smile long gone, Santiago put his hands through his hair before resting them at the base of his neck. "When the U.S. law enforcement proved powerless to save these women and the Mexican government was uncooperative, I felt burdened by the need. I began to pray that God would show me what to do. Soon after that, I was working on a case that put me in contact with Jorge. That's when I learned that his greed superseded everything else for him. And so, I prayed that God would move and work through me."

Uncertain of what to say or how to feel, Violet just listened, standing still and void of any reaction to his words. When he paused, looking for some reaction from her, she nodded for him to continue.

"While I prayed, I got in contact with a rescue ministry in the States. I learned a lot about human trafficking and how important follow-up is. It's one thing to rescue someone, but it's another to actually help them learn how to live a different life than what they were rescued from. Many of the girls working the streets have nothing else; no family, no schooling, no options." Compassionate tears formed in his eyes, and the depth of his concern moved Violet. "I asked if I could partner with this ministry.

I would physically rescue, and they would emotionally and spiritually restore. The first time I offered to purchase a girl from Jorge, I thought he would kill me right then and there. But as I watched him greedily count the money, I knew God had placed me in Tijuana for a reason. I took a break from working with the police and became a private investigator during that time, but eventually I went back to being a police detective. My desire is to figure out a way to safely rescue women without needing large sums of money, or placing my loved ones in danger. That's why I let you think I was bad; it was too risky to be with you. I knew you wouldn't be safe with me as long as I was connected to Jorge. But that's over now."

As Santiago continued to pour out his heart and the details of his history in law enforcement and then working as a rescuer, Violet knew he was telling the truth. All the details fascinated her, and his humility over the amazing, heroic things he had done shocked her. Santiago was a man who was sensitive to God's leading and prompting—he was a man who actually did something about the injustice he saw. And in the midst of it, he had saved her life and then was selfless enough to care more about her safety than defending his character to her.

But what shocked her even more was how Santiago sank down to one knee in front of her. After fumbling in his pocket, he pulled out a small, black velvet box.

Violet's pulse quickened. What was he doing?

Santiago cleared his throat as he opened the box. The sun caught on a ring nestled inside, lighting the diamond solitaire on fire. The ring was simple and modest, but stunningly beautiful.

"Violeta, I love you. I thought I had lost you, but now it's safe to have you back in my life. I'm free now, to build a life with you. I love you more than I ever thought possible. I cannot bear to lose you again. Please, marry me."

Violet couldn't believe what was happening. Didn't sudden proposals like this only happen in the movies?

"I... Santiago... " Violet had a hard time formulating an answer. Kneeling before her was the first man she had ever loved. He was the first man she had kissed and the first one she had shared her dreams with. He held a special place in her heart. But before she could answer him, harsh words broke into the moment.

"What is going on here?" Shawn demanded as he stormed toward Santiago and Violet.

After deftly pushing himself up to stand, Santiago continued to hold the ring out to Violet. "I'm doing what any sane man would do. I'm asking the woman I cherish and love to marry me."

Shawn pursed his lips as he shook his head just the slightest. "I knew it. I should have just stayed here instead of trying to do something romantic."

Violet's eyes widened when she heard the word romantic. *What could he possibly have planned?*

Shawn stared at Santiago. The hostility between the two men was almost tangible. Violet watched with nervousness as Shawn started to say something to Santiago. But suddenly, Shawn turned away from him and leveled his gaze on Violet.

Looking at her with eyes that held tenderness, Shawn reached out his right fist and slowly uncurled his fingers to reveal the engagement ring that once graced Violet's left hand. "Please Vi. Please take this back. Be my wife. Be my future."

Epilogue

The day dawned bright and clear, void of the fog that normally shrouded the coastal town in the early morning hours.

Standing at the large bay window in her parents' living room, Violet couldn't help but smile. The beautiful sunshine pouring in covered her with its warmth and light, causing the engagement ring on her hand to sparkle.

I'm getting married today!

It didn't seem real, but in just a matter of hours, she would no longer be Miss Violet Thompson. The thought filled her with wonder and set butterflies fluttering in her stomach.

Giggling, Violet nearly danced her way into the kitchen to get a cup of coffee. She was so excited she didn't need the caffeine, but just the taste of the strong brew was something she enjoyed.

Tomorrow I'll be drinking coffee with my husband.

Violet laughed out loud—a long, joyful laugh—as she added an extra splash of creamer to her cup. She wanted to celebrate in every way possible and extra rich coffee certainly felt like a fitting indulgence.

Violet studied her fingers as they wrapped around her mug. Rachel had talked her into getting a manicure yesterday, and the carefully sculpted and painted nails looked foreign to her. They did, however, look beautiful and she was glad she had listened to her friend. Hopefully she would feel the same way about the makeup that Rachel insisted she wear. *"You're so beautiful right now without makeup; you'll be flat out the most stunning bride ever, once we add just a touch of lipstick and mascara,"* Rachel's persuasive words still echoed in Violet's memory.

Rachel was so excited to be the matron of honor that Violet couldn't help but let her friend dote on her—even if it meant doing things her practical personality normally didn't see a need for.

Truth, with its heart illuminating and pride removing abilities, struck her deep inside. She had always been so practical, and yet, she'd missed the mark so many times. In her desire to preserve her heart from the same grief her sister had incurred, she had put God in a box. And in her desire to make the most of each moment, serving God in the best way she thought possible, she had put herself in a box as well.

Gratitude coursed through her as she recognized all the growth that had taken place in her heart and mind. *God, I'm beginning a whole new season of life, please let me live this season with greater maturity and spiritual depth than the last season. Help me to stop trying to please you in my own strength, and to realize that what pleases You the most is simply a life laid at Your feet — a willingness to do whatever you ask, whether great or small in our own eyes.*

• • •●• • •

Violet stood in the doorway of the church's sanctuary holding onto the arm of her father. Pulling in a full breath to steady her excited nerves, she looked up into the face of the man who had taught her what real love and commitment looks like. Blinking back joyful tears, she smiled and then snuggled against his arm.

"That dress looks just as beautiful on you as it did on your mother, I'm a blessed man!" Greg Thompson brought a hand up to cup her face. "And God has blessed you with a wonderful man for me to give you to today."

As the music swelled and everyone who sat in the pews stood, Violet took her first step toward her new life.

Looking up on the platform, Violet saw Dan Riley, Rachel's dad and pastor of the church, standing among some of the people she was honored to call friends and family. Rachel and Violet's own mother, Cora, stood to the left of Dan while Shawn and Santiago stood on his right.

Time seemed to slow as she looked into each of their faces. They were all smiling and united in joy. Violet marveled at the work of restoration God had done in the friendship of Shawn and Santiago. The fact that these two men could stand side by side on this day seemed almost like a miracle.

Without much ado, the ceremony began; each moment bringing her closer to saying her vows. Violet's heart hammered in her chest. They had decided to surprise each other with special vows that they had written in secret, waiting to be revealed on their wedding day. *Will my vows mean as much to him as they do to me?*

Squeezing the hand of her soon to be husband, who stood at her side, she snuck a peek at his handsome face. She had to force herself to pay attention to the short sermon Dan was preaching, reminding herself that she had the rest of her life to admire the details of face she would be waking up to each morning.

Everything went by in a blur of excitement and emotion and suddenly Violet was clearing her throat to speak her vows. "I, Violet, take you, Shawn, to be my husband. I promise to love you and nurture you. I look forward to cheerfully letting you lead me and our future children, both physically and spiritually. I promise to encourage and support you. And... " she smiled a spirited smile, "I will listen to you when you are in 'cop mode' knowing that even though it's a *bossy* mode, it's a sign of your love and protection." Violet paused as a tittering of laughter was heard throughout the sanctuary. Violet even laughed herself when she saw Shawn's nose crinkle as he made a silly face at her. "But most of all, I promise to seek God all my days, therefore allowing Him the ability to form me into the wife you need and want."

The end of Violet's vows had caused Shawn to get choked up. Her heart thrilled to see how moved he was. He may be rugged and tough, but underneath it all, he was one of the most tenderhearted men she had ever known.

Pressing his fingertips to his eyes to stop the moisture that was building there, he rocked up onto his tiptoes and back down in a nervous gesture. But as he began to speak his vows, calm confidence pushed past everything else.

"I, Shawn, take you, Violet, to be my wife. I promise to care for you and protect you. I will strive to love you as Jesus loves His church. I stand here before these witnesses, declaring my desire to listen to your wisdom... " Shawn paused here and gave Violet his own spirited smile, "even though you get a little headstrong and pushy at times." Unlike the restrained laughter that Violet's vows got, the laughter that erupted during Shawn's vows was filled with belly laughs. It was no secret that Shawn and Violet would have some lively arguments in their married days, but everyone took joy in the fact that the bride and groom knew each other well enough to include each other's tendency toward bossiness and headstrong actions in the vows. Knowing someone's faults and loving them anyway was far better than trying to claim false perfection.

Once the congregation quieted, Shawn continued. "Violet, when God gave you to me, I was blessed beyond anything I can imagine and I will thank Him every day that I live for the honor of calling you my wife."

The sweet words nourished Violet's soul with their expression of love and genuine desire to be a Godly husband.

Once the vows were taken, the rest of the day passed so quickly that Violet feared she would have trouble remembering the details of the ceremony or the reception that followed.

After Rachel helped Violet out of her wedding dress and into the outfit she had purchased for their "going away," Violet went in search of her husband. When she found him, a sudden shyness enveloped her. In just a moment they would be driving away from the church in Shawn's car. And then, it would be just the two of them, free to do as they pleased and to celebrate the meshing of their two lives into one.

Shawn tugged on Violet's hand, whispering that Santiago was bringing the car around to the front of the church. They were slowly making their way through well-wishers when Santiago walked through the doors. Seriousness marked his face and when Violet saw the angst in his eyes, she gasped. "What? What happened?"

Ignoring her, he turned to Shawn and said, "You've got to see this."

Shawn let go of Violet's hand and sprinted with Santiago for the door, leaving her running to keep up.

When she stepped outside, she heard Shawn barking orders. "Someone get some pictures! Get a crew in here to take finger prints."

His commands alarmed and confused her all at the same time. But when she came closer to the car, she realized that the paint on the windows wasn't the typical message of "just married." Instead, the words written on the windows of the car left her unable to breathe. Feeling violated, she read the words a second time as if she had misread them the first time.

> "coNGratulATions ShAN. MaY You EnJOY thE HAPines You STOle From ME. WilL IT LasT as LonG as You THinK?"

Sinking to the ground, Violet's fingers felt numb and the world spun. *This can't be happening. This just can't be happening.*

Hearing someone come sit next to her, Violet felt strong arms come around her and she smelled the comforting scent of Shawn. "Sweetheart, we can just take your car. I've got capable men handling this."

Violet looked at Shawn as if in a daze. He caressed her face and kissed her brow. "Vi, baby, nothing can ruin this day. Come away with me. Let's celebrate our life together."

Shawn's words helped to clear her head. And in the midst of the chaos around her, she felt God speak to her heart. God had brought them this far, He wasn't going to leave them now.

Standing up, Violet reached out a hand to Shawn as he, too, stood. "Mr. Sinclair, I have the feeling that life with you is going to be anything but boring."

Wrapping her arms around his neck, she savored the feel of his rough, sandpaper cheek against hers. "But whatever comes our way, I know I'll be just fine because I have you and I have God. What more could any woman ask for?"

The Author

As a writer, my biggest desire is to share with others the importance of using our ability to choose, because life can present us with many options. Many of the options out there are negative because the world pressures us to "fit in." If we choose to follow the world, or simply do what feels easiest, we may fail to attain what God has designed for us as individuals.

Each piece of work I present to my readers is designed to encourage people to take a step back and challenge the world's message. There is a purpose that only you can serve, and it's created by God just for you. In the end, it's all about the ability to choose. You can choose the world's plan for your life, or you can choose something more rewarding—God's plan.

My story begins when I was just six years old. My life was forever changed when "The Finley Family" began our full-time, faith based ministry. For 16 years, we traveled across the United States, performing concerts and sharing the love of Christ. During that time I played three instruments, sang, and wrote several songs. My musical talents were truly a gift from God.

Life has a way of changing us and preparing our hearts for the work that God will bring us into later on, and that's exactly what happened when I started teaching a Bible study for young teen girls when I was in my early 20's. It was during this time that I was first introduced to the pain and suffering many teens experience at the hands of people who claim to care about them but don't. Accounts of domestic violence, stalking, and all kinds of abuse were confided to me and I spent time helping these girls, most of whom were in the foster care system, break free from their past and press on to be more than what had been demonstrated for them by their abusers. This season of ministry impacted my heart and has deepened each of my novels, putting a voice to the tragedies seen in this world, and, hopefully, inspiring my readers to be the change the world so desperately needs.

I met my husband, Luke Gertner, when I was twenty-two. His charm and love for the Lord had not only caused him to be well-known in the Southern Baptist Association, it caused me to find him irresistible. After a brief long distance courtship, we married eleven months later.

Once married, I transitioned from my family's ministry into the role of pastor's wife. During this time I completed training to counsel at the Crisis Pregnancy Resource Center in Porterville, California where I was once again the confidante of many abused and hurting women.

In 2006 my husband and I, along with our infant son, moved to Sacramento, California. I enjoyed holding various volunteer positions at the church where Luke was on staff, but the most rewarding parts of my participation at that church was teaching Sunday School for the youth. It was during that time I discovered my love for writing as I wrote my own teaching materials.

In December 2011, Luke was diagnosed with cancer and he fought a valiant fight, spending most of his time witnessing to the medical staff and brainstorming on how he could use his illness to bring glory to God. He succeeded to do both before he left this earth on May 28, 2013.

I now live in a small Oregon town with my family where writing has become an important part of my life. I am currently writing articles for several Christian magazines, and bringing characters to life in The Strength To Stand Series. This collection of four books includes my first novel, *A Different Road Traveled*, which received the Xulon Press First Place Award for Christian Fiction, 2014. Check out www.TheStrengthToStand.com for more information on the award and the books in the series.

You can also find some of my work on Facebook! Go to *I Choose Joy* and like my page to see the weekly posting of encouragement and lessons God is teaching me as I journey through life.

I would like to thank you for taking the time to read not only my creative works, but this biography as well. You, too, have a unique story and I would encourage you to share it! I always enjoy hearing from my readers; you can write to me and share with me how God has encouraged you through this book by emailing me at info@rebeccagertner.com.

May God bless and strengthen you for the work He has for you!

Study Questions

- In what ways do you relate to Violet Thompson?

- Upon her arrival in Mexico the second time, Violet was informed that she wouldn't be able to serve in the way she thought she would. This information bothered her because she felt one ministry was better than the other. In what ways have you had a similar experience?

- How could Violet have handled her relationships better?

- Was Violet's secrecy necessary? Describe a time in your life when you felt the need for secrecy when in reality, sharing the truth was by far the best choice.

- Attempting a rescue is incredibly dangerous and should only be handled by people who have been extensively trained for those situations. In order to insure both you and the victim are as safe as possible, what would you do if you were faced with needing to help someone escape a dangerous situation like Violet was when Misty sought her out for help?

- If you were to be asked about your convictions concerning human trafficking and sex trafficking, what would you say?

Human Trafficking and Sex Trafficking

Human Trafficking and Sex Trafficking are bigger problems than most people realize. They are epidemics that are sweeping through every nation and country.

This new form of slavery is heartbreaking; and just as equally heartbreaking is the serious lack of knowledge concerning this terrible problem, resulting in a lack of action to eradicate this injustice. It's very likely that each of us have come into contact with someone stuck in trafficking and just didn't know it.

While there are many indications that indicate someone is being subjected to trafficking, there are some things that serve as red flags.

These red flags include:

- Someone is required to live with their employer.
- They live in poor living conditions with multiple people in a cramped space.
- You are not able to speak with an individual alone.

- The person's answers appear to be scripted and rehearsed.
- The employer is holding identity documents.
- Signs of physical abuse are present — visible bruises and injuries, or odd behaviors such as wearing long sleeves during summer and sunglasses while indoors.
- You witness submissive or fearful behaviors toward their employer.
- You witness an employee who is unpaid or paid very little.
- You observe someone who is under the age of 18 and in prostitution.

Like the above list mentions, most often, you will not be able to speak with the person you are concerned about. But if you can, here are some questions that might prove helpful:

- Can you leave your job if you want to?
- Can you come and go as you please?
- Have you ever been hurt or threatened because you tried to leave?
- Has your family been threatened?
- Where do you sleep and eat?
- Are you in debt to your employer?
- Do you have your passport/identification in your possession?

If you suspect someone is in a trafficking situation, alert law enforcement immediately. Never attempt a rescue as it may be unsafe for you and the trafficking victim. You have no way of knowing how the trafficker may react and retaliate against the victim and you.

If a victim has escaped a trafficking situation, there are a number of organizations to whom the victim could be referred for help with shelter, medical care, legal assistance, and other critical services. Your local police station should have the information concerning these organizations.

Disclaimer:

These information resources are presented for you to read, assimilate, and pursue only if you believe they are important to you. You bear full responsibility for your assessment and application, if any, of any of these resources. These resources are actions or recommendations of actions the author believes may be helpful, and strictly represent her own opinions. These resources may or may not represent the opinions of anyone involved in the production of this book. In no way do these resources represent any legal opinion or legal counsel whatsoever. Do not use these resources apart from seeking professional assistance from police authorities, professional counselors, licensed medical servicing personnel, or legal counsel. Author and all parties engaged in the production of this book bear no responsibility whatsoever for any outcomes of your situation whether these resources are or were used or not. If you feel you are the victim of trafficking or you believe you have come in contact with people who are victims of trafficking, contact your local police department or other professional personnel.

Products and Services

Unstoppable Truth

A 30-Day Devotional

Rebecca Gertner

The message of truth that the world has to offer has been mixed with half-truths, lies, and hidden agendas. It's a dangerous kind of truth that needs to be stopped from influencing our lives.

The message in this book, however, is God's truth — truth that rightfully deserves full reign of our hearts and minds. It has the power to positively affect your earthly life and when embraced, results in eternal life.

God's truth is an unstoppable force. Nothing can stop it, not silence, not denial, not even death. We can either choose to be a part of it, or we can stand back and watch it move powerfully in the lives of others.

Unstoppable Truth will provide you with 30 devotionals designed to challenge you to fully embrace God's truth, allowing its unstoppable greatness to work in you.

The Strength To Stand Series

Books by Rebecca Gertner

In a world where standing for your beliefs and being boldly different takes courage and strength, it's tempting to settle for average. But for the main characters of *The Strength to Stand Series*, breaking out of the mold is just part of their everyday existence.

As Rachel Riley, Violet Thompson, Mercy Taylor, and Shawn Sinclair seek to accomplish the things they feel driven to live for, they each face heartache and pain. And for some, the results include their very existence being placed in jeopardy.

In the midst of it all, each one finds that true satisfaction in life is only obtained through being an overcomer and standing strong. They discover for themselves that anything worthwhile is worth the risk.

Find yourself inspired and encouraged to be all you were meant to be as you are immersed into the difficulties and triumphs of the courageous people who dared to be different.

*****

A Different Road Traveled
Book One

Xulan Press First Place Award for Christian Fiction, 2014

What happens when obtaining the dreams of one person means the death of another person's dreams?

Rachel Riley is a strong woman. She's a woman who knows what she wants from life. She's beautiful, independent, and successful.

Frank Smith is a strong man. He's a man who knows what he wants from life. But he doesn't know how to get it. And after many failures, he's convinced that fulfillment is just around the corner.

In this gut wrenching drama of clashing desires, Rachel Riley faces her worst fears while Frank Smith deals with his own demons that are dragging him down. As they both fight for what they want, they will have to turn to something stronger than themselves to help them live their dream life.

With a refreshing mix of humor and drama, this book will have your heart pounding in fear and your mouth shouting in anger, all while laughing at the unique personalities of the people captured on the page. But most of all, it will inspire you to find the strength to live the life you want. But choose wisely... what gives you strength now may be your undoing later.

*****

A Different Life Lived
Book Two

What happens when keeping a secret is harmful to one person's life, but revealing the secret could bring the end to someone else's?

When Violet Thompson decides to return to Mexico, she thinks it will be a good thing. But when it costs her a relationship she thought she wanted, she begins to wonder. Then, when the missions trip involves something she didn't expect, she finds herself faced with the decision to pack up and go home, or to face her fears and press on.

Will Violet be able to keep her secret? Or will she have to risk the life of someone else in order to save her own?

*****

Coming soon…

A Different Child Born
Book Three

When faced with danger, how do you decide which action is the lesser of two evils?

For Mercy Taylor, it seems as if every choice she makes will end in sorrow. With a tragic childhood and a marriage that ended too soon, it comes as no surprise that she finds herself fighting for her life. But the traumatic events of her life include more than just herself this time, they include her child as well.

As she is literally running from her past, she's forced to make decisions she's not prepared to make. But in order to make the right choice, she must come to terms with her past and find a source of hope for the future.

*****

Coming soon…

A Different Plan Unfolding
Book Four

What happens when your future is threatened?

For Shawn Sinclair, the answer to that question demands to be found as he watches his world crumble before his very eyes. With just three little words, his life will never be the same, and fear begins to consume him.

While Shawn braves his worst nightmare, his wife is left to pull the pieces of their shattered dreams back together in a desperate attempt to keep from falling into the deep pit of depression that promises escape.

Will Shawn and his wife find a way to keep the life they so desperately want?

*****

I Choose Joy

I Choose Joy is a Facebook blog about one woman's journey through life and her desire to remain joyful and radiant regardless of her circumstances.

Join the Facebook crowd today by going to *I Choose Joy* by Rebecca Gertner and click "like" to see all the encouraging devotional and life-lesson posts!

If you don't use Facebook, you can still be part of the *I Choose Joy* following. Simply send an email to info@rebeccagertner.com and ask to be added to the email list and have the postings sent directly to your email inbox!

*****

Speaking Engagements

Rebecca Gertner is available to speak at your next conference or event! For more information, please send an email to **info@rebeccagertner.com**.

CPSIA information can be obtained at www.ICGtesting.com
Printed in the USA
BVOW04s2351210714

359953BV00002B/67/P